MAY   2002

THAT'LL DO, MOSS

THAT'LL DO, MOSS

BETTY LEVIN

GREENWILLOW BOOKS
An Imprint of HarperCollins Publishers

Mike Canaday and Sue Schoen, V.M.D., kindly assisted
with background material for this book.

Library of Congress Cataloging-in-Publication Data

Levin, Betty.
That'll do, Moss / by Betty Levin.
    p.   cm. "Greenwillow Books."
Sequel to: Look back, Moss.
Summary: During the summer that Diane lives with a family
as their babysitter, she works to establish rapport with the
border collie Moss as everyone tries to cope with several crises.
ISBN 0-06-000531-9 (trade).
ISBN 0-06-000532-7 (lib. bdg.)
[1. Border collie—Fiction.   2. Dogs—Training—Fiction.
3. Babysitters—Fiction.   4. Rabies—Fiction.
5. Maine—Fiction.]   I. Title.
PZ7.L5759 Th 2002   [Fic]—dc21   2001045134
1   2   3   4   5   6   7   8   9   10
First Edition

To handlers and sometime traveling companions on journeys to the trials:

> Carol Campion
> Michael Dathe
> Lynn Deschambeault
> Ed Hobart
> Jean Kennedy
> Bev Lambert
> Tom Leigh
> Denise Leonard
> Maurice MacGregor
> Ellen Raja
> Sue Schoen
> Steve Wetmore

PROLOGUE

It has no conscious selfhood, no knowledge of its origins. Sometimes called Lyssa, its kind has inhabited the earth since the dawn of time. Without memory, it cannot mourn the loss of those whose lives it has shared. Fearless, driven, it seeks out a living shelter to which it becomes attached. There, for a while, it is nourished, fulfilled. But only for a while. Each dwelling is like a tree hosting termites that devour the wood from within. Each dwelling must be sacrificed so that another Lyssa generation may thrive. There is no malice in this exchange, no deadly intent. Simply, it is Lyssa's nature to move on, to be replenished. And almost every host that serves this end, regardless of size and vigor, is doomed.

1

Later, much later, Diane would think back to that Friday afternoon in May and imagine how things might have turned out if only she had noticed more. No, not noticed but paid serious attention to what she saw.

That day she was the last off the bus and the only one to turn onto the steep side road that led to the Ragged Mountain Garden Center. Once again she would be spending the weekend with the Prager family to help look after the two boys. Could she find a little time for herself, too? Homework wasn't the only thing on her mind.

Trudging uphill, her head a tangle of thoughts, she found herself walking straight into a major mess. What stopped her cold was the stink, unmistakable even from a distance.

The moment she caught sight of the skunk ahead of her she could tell that something was really weird about it. She might have turned back if she hadn't already heard the school bus roar off along the main road.

With nowhere else to go, she jumped into the roadside ditch and waited for the skunk to leave. Even though she had extra clothes in her backpack for the weekend, she wasn't taking any chances. It was common knowledge that if you ever got a direct hit from a skunk, everything you were wearing and carrying would have to be thrown out or burned. So she kept her eye on the skunk while she clambered onto the high ground on the far side of the ditch.

But the skunk was in no hurry to move on. It waddled aimlessly, then suddenly rushed at a shadow, snapping at something Diane couldn't see. It twirled as if possessed by demons. After that it staggered dizzily, and then it halted, its mouth agape.

Diane took note of its sharp little teeth. An image from several years before flickered through her thoughts, a picture of a rabid raccoon that had been displayed in school to warn everyone of the danger. But the rabies scare had died down, and no one talked about it anymore. Besides, this was just a skunk playing some kind of game. Maybe it was pretending to be ferocious. The thing to worry about wasn't its bite but its spray.

Jace came biking up the hill.

"Watch out!" she called to him. "There's a skunk up ahead."

"You're afraid of a skunk?" He sounded almost gleeful.

She shrugged. Ever since the day they had walked up the road together and he had warned her about the Pederson ghost, he kept trying to prove to her that he was tough. She hadn't even known that there was a house at the end of what she supposed was an abandoned path until Jace had moved to the middle of the road to give the overgrown driveway a wide berth. "Everyone knows," he had informed her. "That man, that Axel Pederson, he never left the place. It's where he died. His ghost won't leave either. That's why no one lives there."

Diane had assumed he was kidding. How could a guy like Jace, who was old enough to earn a regular salary at the garden center, actually believe such garbage? When she made the mistake of speaking her mind, Jace's face had set in sullen resentment. Since then he had biked to work. And when he couldn't avoid her at the garden center, he would find some way to remind her that even if they did ride the same bus on Fridays, high school was a world apart from middle school, and she was nothing more than a glorified baby-sitter.

"The thing is," Jace declared as he came abreast of her, "if you're quick enough, a skunk can't back up and aim at you." He hunched his lanky body over the handlebars and pedaled past her.

But farther along he slowed. Then he headed toward the skunk, egging it on. Diane figured he was showing off for her benefit. When the squat black-and-white animal really did dash at him, he hooted with mock alarm and fled. The little beast charged the bike's rear wheel, but Jace was clear of it. All he had to do was turn off the road into the garden center.

Diane scowled as she tried to rearrange the image of a skunk attacking a bike. Or did it just look like an attack? Maybe the skunk was injured. Being in pain could make it act crazy. She stifled an impulse to go in for a closer look.

Barely in time, too. A car, speeding down the road, seemed to appear from nowhere. Just when it was about to pass the entrance to the garden center, it suddenly braked, and something was tossed out the front window on the passenger side. An animal? A live animal? Yes, a cat. As it skittered toward the woods, Diane caught a clear glimpse of it. A cat, low-slung with a swollen middle. Was it going to have kittens? Was that why it had been dumped?

The car lurched forward, then had to swerve to avoid the skunk. But the frantic little beast ran full tilt at it, jaws snapping at a front tire. Somehow the driver managed to steer around it. Still, the skunk had no fear. Once again it hurled itself at the car. Diane heard an awful thump as a rear wheel hit. The car kept going, picking up speed as it passed Diane and headed downhill.

She waited a moment longer, peering at the black-and-white mound of fur. What if the skunk wasn't dead, only maimed? What if it was suffering? What if it blamed the next thing it saw, which would be her?

Keeping to her side of the road, holding her breath against the skunk smell, she drew closer. It took only one quick glance to confirm that there was no sign of life. The feisty little skunk was nothing now. It was road kill.

Where was the cat? If it wandered into the garden center, some kind soul might take it home. At least it hadn't been skunked. Not smelling awful would improve its chance of being adopted.

Should she go looking for it? But if it was scared, wouldn't it run and hide? For all she knew it was already up a tree. She glanced at the bare branches casting a fretwork of shadows over the dead skunk. At least the cat was alive. If the poor thing wanted to be with people, it would show up on its own terms.

Still gazing upward, Diane caught sight of a crow banking down the sky. Spying the skunk remains, it uttered a single croak, flapped its shiny black wings, and dropped to the road.

2   Friday afternoons were wildly busy, the new garden center packed with customers buying seedlings to plant over the weekend. Janet and Rick Prager juggled requests and sales, several at a time. Even their boys fetched and carried.

Only Moss, the black-and-white Border Collie, was motionless. That is, he lay beside the stacked bags of buckwheat hulls, looking like a statue, until he saw Diane. Then he sprang to his feet and came weaving between the people to greet her. His muted gladness made her happy and sad: happy because it reflected an understanding they already shared, sad because it paled beside his past exuberance.

Jace, already at work, was trying to hoist a young sapling onto a pickup bed. As Moss dodged around the balled root, Jace scowled at him for getting in the way. "Just don't go messing with the skunk on the road," he grumbled.

Speaking over the dog's head, Diane told Jace the skunk had been run over. Janet, who never missed anything paused long enough to send Jace off with a shovel so customers wouldn't be holding their noses all weekend.

But he came right back because there wasn't enough left to bury. "Crows got it," he said. "And some other animal, I think. Back there in the woods."

Diane started to say something about the cat, but no one was listening to her. She squatted down close to Moss. "I'm glad that animal wasn't you," she murmured. It was sickening to think that the cat was hungry enough to fight a crow for the disgusting remains of a skunk.

Moss leaned against her. Even though he was glad to see her, the spark inside him that had burned so brightly at last year's sheepdog trials had dimmed. "You'd better go lie down again before someone else decides you're in the way," she told him. She pointed to the buckwheat hull bags, and he returned to his place.

"I want to see the skunk," Steven said to her.

"Me, too," said Tim.

"You'd freak out," Steven said to his younger brother. "It'll be gross."

"It's just a dead skunk. Or was," Jace told the boys.

Janet said, "You kids stay off the road unless there's an adult with you."

"Is Diane an adult or a kid?" Steven asked her.

"You know what I mean, Steven," his mother said a bit sharply. "I don't have time for this right now."

Steven turned to Diane. "What did the skunk look like?"

"You know," she told him. "Black with a white stripe."

"Moss is black with a white stripe on his face," said Steven, "but he's a Border Collie. Anyway, I know what a live skunk looks like. That's not what I mean."

Hearing his name, Moss rose again, then watched intently as a car pulled into the parking area. He tensed, looking the way he would if he were about to be sent to gather sheep or cows. But as soon as the car's driver and passengers emerged, his head dropped and he settled back in his spot.

At closing time, as Jace walked his bike to the gate, another car pulled off the road and stopped. The driver leaned out of the window and said, "Good evening. I'm Ralph Slade. My wife and I are buying the property down-hill, the Pederson place. We're your future neighbors. I don't mean to hold you up." But he got out of the car and stood beside it while the Prager family and Diane and Jace gathered to meet him.

"The Pederson place!" exclaimed Janet, brushing back her cropped brown hair. "No one's lived there for years."

"I can tell," Ralph Slade replied. "Actually I've been all the way to the house only once, and once was enough."

"You think it can be restored?" Rick asked.

"Oh, no. It's rotten through and through. No, we'll get rid of it and start fresh. We're going to build the retirement home of our dreams."

Jace stared at Ralph Slade, then cast his eye from Rick to Janet. Finally he turned to look at Diane, who refused to meet his gaze. "Don't you know?" he blurted.

Diane cringed. He was about to warn this newcomer about the ghost.

Rick said, "I think Jace is bitten by the haunted house bug. When I was growing up here, the house was off limits. But once in a while older kids lured us there and then scared the daylights out of us."

Mr. Slade laughed and said, "Every derelict house must get a reputation. When it's gone and the place is cleaned up, kids will have to look somewhere else for a thrill."

"Not just kids," Jace muttered under his breath.

Mr. Slade said, "What?"

Jace caught a look from Rick. He shook his head. "Nothing," he said.

Ralph Slade said to Rick, "I hope you'll be able to help with landscaping. We'll be starting from scratch."

Rick said he'd be glad to oblige, but he'd have to wait for the old house to be demolished and the new one built.

Mr. Slade shook his head. "See, my wife collects antiques, so she wants to build a replica of the old house. We'll work from measurements and photos. If you'd have a look some time before the bulldozer goes in, maybe for a start you could mark the trees that ought to be spared."

Moss sidled up to the car and peered inside. "Want to come home with me?" Mr. Slade asked him, sounding friendly. But when he reached down to touch the black head, Moss ducked aside and went to stand behind the boys.

As Mr. Slade got in his car and drove out to the road, Rick remarked with an edge in his tone, "Someday that dog will get himself stolen again."

Janet said, "He keeps looking for someone. I wish we knew what's going on inside his head. If only he could tell us where he was all the months he was gone."

"Maybe he was here the whole time," Jace said, mounting his bike. "Maybe the ghost got ahold of him."

"Jace," Janet warned, "we can do without that kind of talk. . . ." She nodded toward Steven and Tim. "Anyhow, Moss wasn't holed up anywhere near us. He was lost."

"Not exactly lost," Diane reminded her. "Someone had him. Someone real," she added, raising her voice. But Jace was already out of earshot.

Janet nodded. "And now he's like a visitor, a polite visitor who can't quite hide his desire to go home."

"Getting to be more trouble than he's worth," Rick muttered.

Diane heard the disapproval in his voice. So did Moss, whose ears flattened as he followed slowly behind them all.

Diane felt sure that getting Moss sheepherding again would lift his spirits. She longed to try working with him. There was a hitch, though. She couldn't do it without Janet's help, and the whole point of her being here was to keep the boys busy while their parents ran the garden center. So how should she make her pitch? Not when Rick and Janet looked worn out and probably didn't want to think about anything but supper. Maybe tomorrow.

3 As soon as Diane heard Janet and Rick stirring, she was up like a shot, upstairs to the bathroom and down again and dressed before they appeared. When she opened the door to let Moss out, there were the two orphan lambs loose among Rick's precious strawberries. Should she send Moss to get them out or wait for Janet to deal with the problem?

The lambs were munching happily. Worse, they were trampling and tearing the delicate plants. She had to do something. But could Moss get them out without making matters worse? Since Janet's dog, Tess, was penned up with her puppies and Moss was at hand, Diane walked him to the end of a space between two rows.

"You listen," she told him. "You listen to me. Come by. Out!" She stood at the edge of the strawberry plot and willed him to bring the lambs straight to her.

Moss leaped over the rows until he straddled some untouched plants behind the lambs. Then he moved toward them with more speed than was called for. At least that was the way it seemed to Diane, who longed to have him complete this small task without mashing anything more. The lambs sprang up on stiffened legs. Diane moved off. One lamb tried to double back, found itself blocked by the dog, and practically flew past the other one and out of the patch. The second lamb followed.

"Slow down," Diane said to Moss as she backed away from the strawberries and he pushed the lambs toward her. He actually paused. Her heart was hammering in her chest.

She kept on backing until she was close enough to the lamb pen to run and open it. The gate was already ajar. She realized that it had never been latched after Steven fed the lambs their last bottle. She was too aghast at the resulting havoc to feel elated over the way Moss had come through for her.

Once the lambs had scuttled inside and she secured the gate, she realized that Rick and Janet were outside surveying the damage.

Rick asked how the lambs had broken out. He said that if

Steven wanted to carry on rearing them, he'd have to take his lamb chores more seriously.

But Diane knew she was at least partly to blame.

Janet said to her, "If you'd check up on this sort of thing . . ."

Diane nodded. "I saw that the gate was closed. I just didn't look that close."

Janet nodded. "The puppies and the lambs need almost as much watching as the boys. You'd better give Steven and Tim breakfast while I help Rick with the strawberries."

Almost as an afterthought, Janet called back to her, "Nice dog handling. You thought before you sent Moss after them. He behaved for you."

Diane felt her face grow warm. This could be the moment to speak up for Moss. If only Janet wasn't in a hurry to repair the strawberry damage, one more task before the garden center opened for the day. Diane let the moment go. She called Moss with her to the house and sent him upstairs to wake the boys.

She didn't have much to do for their breakfast, but she washed up last night's supper dishes while they ate their cold cereal.

"After my birthday I won't be Steven anymore," Steven said.

Diane scarcely heard this remark. But Tim asked, "How come? Will you still be my brother?"

"Of course," Steven told him. "I'm just going to be—" He paused. "I'm going to be someone else."

"Because of your birthday?" asked Tim.

Steven said, "*For* my birthday. And Moss."

Moss! All at once Diane was listening. She said, "Don't be silly, Steven. What do you mean?"

"Mom and Dad asked me what I want. Well, I want a different name, and I want Moss. I want to run him in a trial."

Diane said, "Even if you do get to work Moss someday, he belongs to Zanna."

"She never comes anymore. What's the use of owning something you never see?"

Diane had to stick up for Zanna. They had been best friends before Zanna's family moved to California two years ago. Steven probably didn't remember that when Zanna lived next to his grandparents' farm, she had all but rescued Moss when no one else had time for him. Steven couldn't know how hard it had been for her to leave Moss with Janet so that he could continue to do the work he was trained for. Still, Diane didn't know how to answer the question about owning, so she simply said, "It's not Zanna's fault she can't have Moss. Kids can't choose where they live."

Steven considered this. "You're going to stay here this summer, not just weekends. Right?"

Diane nodded.

"Because you have to?"

He didn't miss much, she thought. Choosing her words with care, she said, "My mom thinks it's a good place to be because it's healthy and safe." She kept to herself what was inside her head, her aunt's blunt assertion that Mom had done right by Diane and now deserved to live her life, too. The message got through to Diane, though. Mom deserved the freedom to take off with Mark on his truck route anytime she could get off work.

Tim said, "I'm glad. It's fun when you're here."

She smiled at him. She said, "Me, too, Tim. I've liked coming ever since last summer, when we went to sheepdog trials together. Remember? And when Zanna visited."

But Tim's memory must be even fuzzier than Steven's. Neither boy realized that in a way Moss was the reason Diane was here with them now. Neither could have known that last year Diane had started coming to them because Zanna had implored her for news about her dog.

It was even less possible to imagine what Moss actually recalled. As Janet had remarked, no one could get inside his head. Of course, some things could be assumed, like his missing Zanna. What was a dog's memory really like? How could Moss understand the tide of affection and loyalty that governed his feelings? Diane supposed that to begin with, she must have reminded him of Zanna. And then what? All Diane could be sure of was that bit by bit she and Moss had warmed to each other.

Then he had disappeared.

By the time Zanna arrived for her long-planned visit, losing Moss, not knowing whether he was dead or alive, had been a crushing blow for both girls.

Long after all hope was gone, Moss had reappeared in time to be reunited with Zanna before she had to leave him again. Everyone had called it a miracle. Diane would never forget their astonishment, the relief spilling into a flood of joy.

Only, what had become of that joy? What had become of Moss?

Steven, who wasn't ready to give up on the ownership question, said, "Moss sometimes acts like my dog."

Diane said, "That's good. It's good for him to belong that way."

Still, she knew it wasn't enough. Moss had a place to stay. He had good care. He even got a bit of work now and then. But mostly he just seemed to be waiting for his life to start up once more.

4 The boys forgot about the skunk until they
went over to the garden center to ask their
mother if they could let the puppies out. Diane had told
them it wasn't a good idea for the puppies to run free with
so many people coming and going. Steven was sure she was
wrong.

The faint skunk odor that wafted over the parking area
gave him an opening. "If it was a mother skunk that got
killed and it had babies and we found them, could we keep
one?" he asked.

Jace laughed. "You adopt a baby skunk, and I'm out of
here."

"There weren't any babies," Diane told Steven. If she
mentioned the mother cat and it never showed up, Steven
would be bugging her about kittens, too.

"So can we take the puppies outside?" He was addressing
his mother now. "We won't lose any."

Janet set down the crate she had been carrying. She
looked past Steven to Diane. "You up for this?"

Diane knew how quickly a pup could slip away once
they were all running about and exploring. She would be
responsible if anything went wrong.

"Diane doesn't want the puppies to have fun," Steven
said.

Diane opened her mouth to protest, then shut it. She
refused to be drawn into a stupid argument with him.

Janet said, "You can let the puppies out as long as all
three of you watch them."

The boys turned to run.

"I mean it," Janet called after them. "Three people
means six eyes, one for each puppy."

Diane wondered if this was the moment to speak for Moss. For herself. But Janet was hoisting up the crate again and shifting it onto a pallet. Maybe when she broke for lunch. Maybe then.

The six puppies swarmed like giant furry bees. One attacked a pot of basil and knocked it over. Another charged into Moss, who growled at it and departed. The next one found the coiled hose and dragged it until it snagged on itself. That left the pair that was tussling on the lawn and the littlest one, the pup they called Tad because Janet said it was like a tiny tadpole with a big heart.

Diane watched Tim pick up this puppy. It dangled from his arms. Going to its rescue, she told Tim to sit down and let the puppies come to him. When one of them climbed in his lap, then he could hold it.

"They don't come," he complained. "They never do."

"That's because you're not gentle," Steven told him. "Like this." Not for the first time he showed Tim how to clasp a puppy.

"Tim will be able to do that when he's bigger," Diane said sympathetically. This was the part of baby-sitting that got on her nerves, supporting both kids at the same time. When Mrs. Dworsky up the road had her grandchildren visiting and Steven was invited to go play with them, everything got easier. Tim, like the smallest puppy, would emerge from the shadow of his brother and for a little while rule the roost.

Diane scanned the lawn and porch, mentally counting one, two, three, four, five— She stopped at five. One was unaccounted for, and it was that one, the littlest. "Where's Tad?" she asked Steven, who was rolling on the grass pursued by three pups.

Diane called Tess, who crawled out from beneath the lilac bush. The puppies, all but the missing one, came rushing to her to nurse.

"Where's your pup?" Diane asked Tess. But with five puppies dragging on her, Tess just looked at Diane as if the answer were obvious.

Diane went searching, first in the flower beds at the side of the house, then to the lamb paddock, and, finally, as squawking commenced, over by the chicken coop. The puppy had squeezed under the gate, and now there was a standoff, the puppy solemnly eyeing the hens and the hens fluffing out feathers and kicking up dust.

As soon as Diane entered the coop, the hens scattered. That seemed to electrify the pup, which shot after them. Diane swooped down to grab it. Even after she picked it up, those running legs kept pumping the air. Diane carried it out of the coop, blocked the gate with a hoe and a rake, and let the puppy go.

She hurried back to check on the others only to find that Steven and another puppy had vanished. "Steven!" she yelled.

"Gone to the bathroom," said Tim.

"Count the puppies," she ordered. As she ran to check in the house, a puppy scrambled out from beneath the porch steps. "Six," she said out loud.

"Five," said Tim.

Steven came outside, looking innocent.

"You promised to stay with the puppies," Diane told him.

"I did. But I had to go."

"So now we put them away," she said.

"It's not their fault," Steven replied. "You're being mean."

Diane sank down on a porch step and groaned. "Count the puppies, please," she said to him. "Tim only got to five."

"Tim doesn't know how to count," Steven told her.

"I do so," Tim retorted. "Next year I'll be in kindergarten, and then I'll read, too."

Steven said, "Or maybe when you get to first grade. Though some kids don't really get reading till second grade." He marched around the yard, counting at the top of his lungs. He counted a second time. "Five," he finally announced. "Tad is missing."

Diane rose to her feet, called Tess out from under the lilac, and then changed her mind. "Moss," she shouted. "Moss, come."

He came loping from the garden center and stood before her with his expectant look. "Pup, pup, pup," she called, and five puppies scurried over. "Puppy, pup, pup," she said more softly to Moss. "Look!" she said. "Moss, get him!"

Moss trotted off.

"He won't do it," Steven said. "He doesn't do finding stuff like that. Besides, you're giving him the command for when a cow or a sheep charges him. You say, 'Get 'em,' to make Moss dive in and, like, attack." He grinned suddenly. "You should see him with the vacuum cleaner. All you have to do is open the closet door and say, 'Get 'em,' and he goes for it like it's some kind of dragon. Dad says if we do it anymore, we'll need a new vacuum cleaner."

Knowing Steven was right about the attack command made her only more determined to prove him wrong about Moss's willingness to look for the puppy. "Good boy, Moss," she said. "Look. Pup, pup, pup. Moss, look!"

Moss tried the chicken coop, the machine shed, and the

barnyard. Then he came back to Diane. But she repeated the words *look* and *pup* until he turned away again, this time heading for the main barn. Instead of following him, she began to gather up the five puppies to put them safely away in their pen.

She was just scooping up the last of them when Moss returned again, this time with the sixth puppy dragging behind him and panting hard. When it flopped down and tried to stretch out on the lawn, Moss nudged it to its feet.

"Good boy!" she told him. Gloating would only make matters worse with Steven, so she said no more. But she dropped to her knees to throw her arms around the dog. Moss responded gravely, leaning against her for a brief moment, his tail slowly waving.

Then he left for the garden center. Diane supposed he would spend the rest of the day watching the cars that drove in and checking on each person who stepped out of them.

5

The grown-ups barely stopped for lunch, but Jace showed up, famished as usual. Taking over the kitchen, he helped himself to any meat leftovers he could find in the refrigerator and huge globs of mayonnaise, which he slathered on both slices of bread. His sandwich making fascinated the boys, who naturally decided that they wanted sandwiches just like Jace's.

Diane, who had been rehearsing her plea for working with Moss, tried not to snap at them. Instead she told Jace not to expect her to clean up after him.

With his mouth full, he merely grunted. Then, after he

had gobbled up his sandwich, he said, "That house, the Pederson place, you won't want to be near there when they tear it down."

"Why not?" asked Steven.

"Because of what's inside. I don't care what Rick thinks. Knock down the house, and it'll come out."

Tim gulped. "What? What'll come out?"

Jace pushed back his chair. "A ghost. The ghost of Axel Pederson that lived there."

"Jace!" Diane said. "You want to scare Tim?"

"He ought to be scared," Jace went on. "You're from town, so you've no idea. But it's common knowledge around here."

"I've never even seen the house," said Steven. "Did you go inside?"

"I was up close," Jace replied. "Close enough to hear, like, this moaning."

"So you saw it?" Steven demanded.

"Didn't have to. There's lots of things won't show themselves to just anyone. Doesn't make them any less dangerous than what we can see." With that, he rose, downed the last of his root beer, and left the house.

"Thanks a lot," said Diane after him. "Thanks a bunch." She stared at the mess he had left behind on the counter and table. Then there was the other mess, the one inside the boys' heads. Which of them would be the first to wake up in the middle of the night screaming about ghosts?

Steven said, "Jace heard it moan."

"Jace heard something or imagined he did, that's all."

"What does moan sound like?" asked Tim.

Steven made a face and howled, and Tim clapped his hands to his ears.

Diane said, "How many things that moan can you name?"

They began with the wind and mourning doves. Soon they were outshouting each other. At least for a while the ghost menace was laid.

The next time trouble loomed, though, Diane knew she might not be able to steer the boys away from it. The hardest part of mother-helping was having to be so much more grown-up than she was at home hanging out with her friends. If she were working like this around town, she'd be checking in with those who also did regular baby-sitting, and they'd compare notes. Out here she couldn't very easily gab on the Pragers' telephone about Steven and Tim.

Anyway, it wasn't clear whether she was supposed to be sort of hired help or something like an older sister to the boys. Not that Diane was all that experienced in the sister department. Sometimes her cousin Connie seemed sisterly. But Connie was graduating from high school this year and had a serious boyfriend. While she seldom acted superior to Diane the way Jace did, she wasn't much interested in doing stuff with her younger cousin anymore.

Diane was pondering all this when the boys' great-grandmother telephoned to ask if she could borrow the dog. Diane was quick to offer her services as well.

Fennella said, "I think Janet is counting on you to look after the boys."

Diane said, "I bet she'd be glad to have them away from here for a while. They love visiting the farm." Did they? Of course they must.

The last thing she wanted was to drag the two boys over to the farm against their will and then have to spend the whole time entertaining them instead of getting in on the dog work, whatever it was.

Fennella asked if Janet was nearby. Diane said she would find her and have her call back.

"How would you guys like to go to the farm this afternoon?" Diane said to the boys as she headed for the garden center.

"Why?" asked Steven suspiciously. "To stay? It's too sad there now."

Diane knew he was thinking about his great-grandfather Rob, who had died the past winter. She said, "Your great-grandmother sounded busy, not sad. She needs a dog. Maybe we all could go. What do you think?" If Steven was already on her side, it would help persuade Janet that they should go along with Moss.

But Janet was too harried to consider anything beyond Fennella's request. "I don't have time to take Moss over there right now," she said as she strode to the house. "Unless it's an emergency, like last time."

It was at this point that Tim spoke up. "Can we go to the farm?" he asked. "Can we? Diane can take care of us."

Janet went inside to call Fennella. When she came back out, she said to Diane, "My grandmother's coming for Moss. My brother has the farm dog with him at his herdsman job, so they're really strapped. But she says she'll take the boys if you go along, too. Heifers broke out of a pasture. It's not the first time they've wandered off."

Diane tried not to sound too eager. She said, "Maybe I can help with Moss."

Janet gave her an appraising look. "Maybe you can. That would be great, Diane. Thanks."

Diane nodded. If things worked out today, it would be only natural to try something more ambitious with the dog.

What she didn't bargain for, though, was the effect on Moss of being on the farm again. All at once he looked eager, hopeful. For what? Diane wondered. Did he know he would be sent for wandering cows?

Fennella eyed him. "Looking for Rob, maybe," she said shortly. It was the first time Diane had heard her mention her husband's name. "Or possibly Zanna," Fennella added. "Of course, the dog associates them both with this place."

Diane couldn't think of a reply. She ought to say she was sorry about Rob, but she didn't know how to.

As Janet's father crossed the road, the two boys ran to meet him. He paused to lift them both from the ground before coming up to Fennella, each grandson still hanging from an arm.

"So you've got the dog," he commented. "Want me to take him?"

Diane vaguely recalled that Janet's parents, Gordon and Dot, didn't much care for Moss.

Fennella shook her head. "Not with your short fuse," she told him. "Moss works somewhat for me. And I'll take Diane along, if you or Dot mind the boys."

Gordon looked doubtful. "It could be pretty rough back there," he warned.

Fennella said, "It's the dog that'll be running, not me. We'll give it a try, anyway."

Gordon looked at Diane. "Zanna's friend," he said. It wasn't a question, but she nodded. She had a feeling he was comparing her with Zanna. Was he trying to figure out how useful she might be? Or was he wondering whether she had learned anything about working a sheepdog? Zanna had been close to this family, especially to Rob, who had shared his beloved Moss with her. Back then they had scarcely known Diane.

Fennella said, "You boys go with your grandfather. Show them the new piglets," she told Gordon. "We'll catch up with you later."

Following Fennella through the gate to the back pasture, Diane found that she had to move right along to keep up. Nothing about Fennella fitted Diane's assumptions about old people. The resemblance between this slight, vibrant woman and Janet was so striking that age comparisons seemed meaningless. It wasn't just the way Fennella's worn jeans and tattered jacket covered her wiry frame. It was Fennella's assured pace, with a brief word for Moss when he veered away from her path and otherwise no talk at all.

Diane scrambled along, her own confidence sliding away as she hurried after the old woman and the dog.

 The pasture dropped steeply to a brook that ran a jagged course across the lower slope of the grazing land. Long before they reached the water, Diane's sneakers were soaked.

"Should've fitted you out with boots," Fennella said ruefully.

"It doesn't matter," Diane answered. She had a feeling that Fennella faulted her for not seeing to her own feet. "They'll dry out," Diane added. She had to concentrate on Moss, on the challenge ahead, and hope that she didn't make any major mistakes.

"There's where they got out," Fennella said, pointing to a section of fence where the wire was mashed. A freshly cut tree limb lay beside it. "Happens every spring," she went on. "Only this year I wasn't right on top of it the way I usually am. The heifers got out a week or so ago and came back of their own accord, so I figured I could wait awhile. They must've heard me down here with the chain saw, but they're taking their own sweet time. They don't know about coyotes and bear. At least," she added, "I hope they don't."

By the time Fennella and Diane reached the fence, Diane's sopping jeans were clinging to her knees. She glanced enviously at Fennella in her high rubber boots.

Fennella spoke to Moss. "Get out," she told him. "Away out."

Moss raised his head, ears erect, eyes eager, and stared into the dense blueberry swamp below the fence. He didn't move.

"Go on, Moss," she ordered. "Away. Out."

Moss glanced to his right and turned uphill.

"No," Fennella said. "Not the sheep." She bent, took his collar, and turned him toward the swamp.

Diane said, "Could I try?"

"Be my guest," said Fennella. "You think he'll work for you?"

Diane had no idea. This was home ground for Moss. He might be listening for voices from his past. He could shut her out entirely. She clambered over the downed fence. "Moss," she said, not daring to command him in case he refused to obey. He followed her, though.

As soon as they were a few yards inside the swamp, she spoke his name again and squatted down beside him. "Look," she whispered to him. "Look back."

He leaped away from her, ran wide along the edge of the swamp, and then turned sharply, sailed over the fence, and veered again up the hill.

"No!" she shouted. "That'll do, Moss. Come!"

He trotted slowly back to her, his ears flattened, his tail between his legs.

Fennella said dryly, "He never has worked for just anyone. He and Zanna forged a bond, if you know what I mean. Besides, they had Rob between them." She fell silent.

Stung, Diane said, "I know that. But Moss does sometimes work for me." She should never have started this. If Moss let her down now, if he blew her off, he might do it again. And again. Who needed that?

To her surprise, Fennella said, "So keep trying. Walk him toward where you want him to go; then send him."

"Moss," Diane said to the dog. She couldn't believe she was letting herself in for another failure. "Come on," she told him. The moment he glanced uphill, she spoke more sharply than she'd intended. "No!" Then she softened her voice. "Here, Moss. With me."

He walked beside her. She followed a muddy path probably made by the heifers. It was rough going. Moss stayed at her heels. Then the ground rose for a spell. It was still slimy, but her feet didn't stick in the muck. Despite the mass of woody shad crowned with tiny white blossoms, there were a few more openings in the undergrowth. She looked down at Moss. He lowered his nose, sniffing. Good, she thought. Maybe cow droppings would give him the idea.

This time, as soon as she sent him, she told him he was good and right. Was he? For an awful moment she thought he was curving back into the pasture and up the hill. But he simply ran wide and disappeared into the forest swamp.

He was on his way. Even if he didn't bring back the wandering heifers, at least he would have tried. For her.

After a while she retraced her steps and returned to Fennella, who had placed sections of the cut tree limb on the low part of the fence to hold it down for the cattle.

They waited. Moss was on what Janet called a blind outrun, which meant that the livestock he had been sent to gather were out of sight. Diane looked at her watch. This gather might take awhile.

Once before, about a year ago, she had sent Moss like this, and he hadn't returned. It had been dark that time. There had been coyotes. Janet said she would have done exactly the same thing. But Diane could never shake off the conviction that she was to blame. Months later, when Moss finally showed up scarred but sound, all the uncertainty and grief ended for everyone—except Diane.

He was taking too long. Even though it wasn't dark like before, these woods alive with spring birdsong might harbor some hidden danger. Maybe she should call him back. Her hands rose to her mouth, though whether to silence herself or to cup her fingers for shouting into the distance, she didn't know.

"Ssh," whispered Fennella. "Hear that?"

Diane strained to listen. If only the birds would stop their racket. At last she heard splashes and breaking branches and, finally, the low grunts and groans of the reluctant herd. Yes, they were coming. Yes! She knew she was grinning like an idiot. She couldn't help herself, relief and triumph surging through her.

As the heifers broke through the bushes, they spread out along the fence. Moss ran from one side to the other, forcing them to regroup. Here Fennella had to take over because Diane didn't know what commands to use. It didn't matter, though. Moss had trusted her when she sent him, he had worked for her when it counted, and nothing terrible had come of it.

Some of the heifers leaped the flattened section of fence, clearing it easily like cows jumping over the moon. Others trod the weighted wire, nervously picking their way. Moss brought up the rear. He was so coated with mud that none of his white markings remained visible. Brambles tangled in his tail prevented him from wagging it when Diane praised him.

Fennella started the heifers up the hill. "We'll move them across the road until I can get the fence repaired," she said. Glancing from Moss to Diane, Fennella added, "Looks like we'll have to take the hose to you as well as the dog."

Diane nodded. She was perfectly willing to wash away all the mud, but she would never be able to wipe the silly grin off her face.

"So no harm done," Janet remarked at supper that night. "All the cows got home safe and sound."

"Except one that got its face scratched," Steven corrected. Janet shrugged. "No big deal. Right?"

Diane said, "It was thick back there. You'd think that more of them would've gotten scratched."

"Grandpa thinks something bit it," Steven told them.

"He was just guessing," Diane said. "Actually he thinks it happened last time they got out. Then branches tore the skin again."

"Bites or scratches?" Rick asked.

Steven wasn't sure. "Grandpa put blue stuff on it, and you couldn't see it anymore."

"The cow looked like a clown," Tim said. "It didn't hurt."

Diane, who hadn't even noticed the bloody marks on the cow's face until after they were in the barnyard, had nothing to add. She was gearing up for her request to work Moss.

She had to wait until the boys were in bed. Rick and Janet settled in front of the television. Within minutes Rick was asleep in his chair. Janet yawned.

Now, thought Diane, who had hoped to be alone with Janet. She said, "Will you be going to sheepdog trials this year?"

Janet turned down the volume on the television. "I'm not sure," she said. "We've sunk an awful lot into the new garden center. We've got to make it pay. That means longer hours, and it's not fair to leave all the weekend work to Rick."

"Won't he have Jace?"

Janet nodded. "But Tess is nursing puppies, so she's far from working fit. I haven't taken her over to the farm for any intensive training. There's never any time."

Diane said as lightly as she could manage, "What about Moss?"

"Oh, Moss," Janet responded. "Well . . ." Her voice trailed off.

Diane said, "He was good today. Really."

Janet nodded. "Farm work's one thing. Trialing calls for more precision, more practice. Moss needs a spring tune-up at least as much as Tess." Muted voices from the television mingled with Rick's gentle snoring.

Diane spoke softly, as if she were interrupting. "I wish I could try. With Moss. I wish I knew how."

"Really?" Janet regarded her. "You don't have to follow in Zanna's footsteps, you know."

Diane thought about this. She said, "The first time I ever tried to work Moss was a disaster. Afterward I thought, never again. Lately we've done a few things that worked. And today was great."

"Today gathering the heifers?"

Diane nodded. "Fennella didn't think Moss would go for me."

Janet laughed. "You showed her, though?"

"Moss showed her," Diane said.

Janet pulled herself up in her chair. "You're really serious," she said. "You're hooked."

"I guess so," Diane answered. "I just never thought I might, you know—" She paused. She didn't want to compare herself with Zanna or Janet. Zanna had a natural talent. Janet had years of experience. What could Diane offer Moss? Nothing, really. Nothing, except maybe she was the only person around here who could see how much he needed to be needed.

Janet said, "I'd be surprised if you hadn't picked up a good deal just coming to trials with me last season. You work hard; you should have fun, too. That's only fair. Well . . ." She let out a slow breath. "Something to sleep on, I guess." Switching off the television, she rose and leaned over Rick. "Come on, my man," she said, shaking him from his deep sleep.

Rick groaned and staggered to his feet. Janet turned out a few lights. Diane spread the bedding bunched at the end of the living-room couch.

She was already undressed when she remembered that Moss was still outside. She scurried to the back door to let him in.

Moss padded into the kitchen. She ran her hand over his coat to make sure that the hose had done its job. Some of the belly and tail and leg hair was still coarse and spiky with embedded mud. By tomorrow morning a layer of silt would be deposited on the floor where he spent the night. Janet didn't mind that sort of thing. Still, Diane was determined to be the first one in the kitchen tomorrow morning. She would let Moss out and then sweep up after him, just as if he had already become her special responsibility.

8 The following Friday Diane tore up the hill from the main road until she ran out of breath. Forced to slow down as she crested the rise, she crossed the road. Wasn't this where the cat had been dumped from the car?

She had been so caught up in plans for Moss that she hadn't given the cat much thought. Guiltily she peered into the woods and listened. What did she expect to hear? Kittens mewing? A cat yowling with hunger? Someone must have picked it up by now. Probably it was happily ensconced in a friendly house, with its litter snuggled close.

Last weekend she had thought about looking for it. Then events had overtaken her. Well, not exactly overtaken, but they had used up Saturday, and Diane had devoted Sunday to being extra-inventive with the boys so that Janet would appreciate how helpful she could be.

Twice during the week Diane had let the opportunity to e-mail Zanna slip by. Tuesdays and Thursdays, Mom's late nights at the supermarket, Diane went to her aunt and uncle's house after school. Her cousin Connie had a computer, which Diane was allowed to use until Connie needed it, and that usually happened before Diane got a reply.

During Zanna's first year in California she and Diane had been in touch all the time. Homesick Zanna had been eager for news about school and friends and Moss. But over the past months she had seemed to lose interest in her old home. This week Diane had been tempted to send her news about Moss, which would almost certainly prompt a response. But what exactly could Diane tell? Like looking for the cat, she had simply done nothing.

Now that she was here again, she called softly, "Kitty, kitty." A squirrel leaped from the wall to a leaning trunk, where it was instantly confronted by another squirrel. The two chased and chattered and then vanished overhead.

No sign of the cat. No sign of last Friday's skunk either. A fresh weekend, a fresh start.

Jace was already at the garden center, and Rick, looking sour, was speaking to him in guarded but firm tones about being prompt and dependable. If Jace didn't shape up, he'd lose his job. Then Janet would be stuck here every weekend.

Janet, who was explaining to a customer the difference between impatiens and double impatiens, waved a greeting in Diane's direction. Tim, soaked from head to toe, came running from behind the raised cold frames. Janet cast Diane a pleading glance.

Steven sauntered into their midst. "Tim asked me to," he said to his mother.

"Let me show you the lavender doubles," she said to the customer.

Diane said to the boys, "Come on. We'll get dry clothes, and then you can show me how much the puppies have grown." Why wasn't Moss here in his usual place? She marched the boys off toward the house.

Moss was tied to the porch. He lay flat and didn't even raise his head at their approach. "Moss," she said. One ear flicked. His chin stayed glued to the ground.

"What's going on?" she asked Steven as she pulled Tim's soaked shirt off.

"I was watering the seedlings like Dad said. Tim wanted—"

"No, I mean, with Moss. Why is he tied?"

Steven said, "He got in someone's car again. They didn't like it. Dad says he might have to stay at the farm. At least they could use him there."

Diane didn't say anything.

Steven seemed to be waiting for her to react. When she didn't, he asked her if she remembered what he'd said about wanting Moss to be his. She nodded. Did he remember what she had told him?

Tim said, "We might keep a puppy. We might keep Tad. To be our own."

Steven said to her, "You have to talk to Dad. Say you'll watch out for Moss. You and me, we can do that."

Diane regarded Steven. She said, "I've already told your mom that I'd like to learn how to work him."

"But I want to," he burst out. "I already said so."

"I know that," Diane told him. "If I learn how to run him, I can show you. We both can do it."

"He won't be mine, though," Steven objected.

"Listen, Steven." Diane knelt and faced him. "He can't be yours. Or mine. But we can still be his friends."

Steven was scowling. "I want to trial him," he muttered.

Diane said, "How about the puppy? He might turn out just like Moss."

"He has to grow up first. Moss is ready to work right away."

"I'll talk to your mom," Diane answered lamely.

"Now? Soon? When?"

"I don't know. Steven, just cool it, or you'll make things worse."

"They're already worse," he grumbled.

"Well, just lay off now," she told him. "Did you mention about changing your name?" she thought to ask him.

"Not yet," he replied.

"Good. Don't."

"Why not?" His voice rose. "What's it got to do with Moss?"

This kid was clueless, she thought. He'd drive anyone up a wall. "Just give your parents a little space," she advised, wondering how far she herself would get.

Tim, in dry clothes, said, "Come see the puppies. See Tad." He scooted down the steps and raced to the pen. Steven followed slowly.

But Diane paused to stroke Moss. She nearly unhitched him, then decided against any move that could lead to trouble with Rick. "Moss," she murmured. The same black ear flicked, signaling that she had made contact.

Over the weekend everything fell into place. Janet and Rick had worked out an arrangement to allow Janet to devote some time each day to lessons for Diane and Moss. Everyone understood that he would become Diane's project as soon as she came for the summer. At least until then, though, he must be tied during the hours the garden center was open.

"Now can I talk about my new name?" Steven whispered to Diane, who was cleaning up after Sunday breakfast.

"Wait a bit," she suggested.

"I already did. I haven't said anything yet."

"We've been working out other stuff," she told him. "Give it a rest."

Steven sighed with impatience. "You talk like a grown-up," he complained.

Diane nodded. There was nothing like a pushy kid to shove you over to the other side.

"What are you two whispering about?" Janet asked as she put down the telephone.

Diane shook her head. Steven glared at her. Tim said, "Steven wants a new name for his birthday."

Janet, on her way out the door, said, "What's wrong with the one you have?"

"Mace," said Steven. "I want to be Mace. Or Ace."

"To rhyme with Jace?" said his mother.

Steven shrugged. He didn't answer.

"Let's talk about it tonight," she said, glancing at her watch. "Your dad's already gone ahead to open the gate."

Steven nodded. He looked relieved to have dodged an immediate *no*. "You see?" he said to Diane. "She didn't get mad."

"Her mind's on other things," Diane said. "She was talking to someone at the farm about maybe going there later to work Moss, to give me a lesson."

"Me, too," Steven told her. "You promised."

Diane said, "I'm not sure we're going, though. She didn't say."

But they did go, after all. Janet waited until the customers slacked off before piling the boys, the two dogs, and Diane into the van.

"You look bone tired," Gordon said when he saw her haul Tim from the car seat. "I hope you and Rick didn't bite off more than you can chew."

"Bite off what?" Tim asked. "What did Mommy bite?"

"It's an expression," Dot, his grandmother, told him from the porch. "And your dad's right," she said to Janet. "You're doing too much. Bringing the yearlings over to your place is only going to add to the burden. Anyway, I thought you were going to start that new herb garden. When will you have time to work the dogs?"

"I'm going to make a little time," Janet answered. "It'll be . . . recreation." She smiled, as if she had made a joke.

Fennella, joining them, said, "If Janet takes the yearling flock, at least she won't have to load up most of the family every time she has a few minutes to spare. I think it makes good sense."

"Well, I guess I can hook up the trailer and bring them tomorrow or the next day," Gordon said. "Will you be ready for them?"

Janet frowned. "Not quite. The fence needs some work. Give me till next weekend."

"You can have as long as you like," Gordon told her. "Take my word for it, you'll find a lot of loose posts."

"I know," Janet said. "The frost heaves them up every spring. I take it there was no problem with the heifers once you got them back," she added.

"Not really," Fennella replied. "Just the one that got torn some. She's not doing that well."

"I thought those were superficial face wounds," Janet remarked.

"Or bites," Steven put in. "Maybe bites."

"It's hard to picture any animal biting like that. A coyote or bear would do more damage. What else would attack a cow head-on?"

Tim said, "They'd bite off more than they could chew?"

"Right you are," Gordon said, laughing. He hoisted up his smaller grandson and swung him onto the porch.

Diane came close to mentioning the skunk she'd seen attacking the wheel of a car. But when she tried to imagine it going after the heifer, she realized that a cow's head was way out of reach. Anyway, what could she tell them about cattle and the perils they faced that these people didn't already know?

She waited for Janet to call the dogs, then followed her past the sheep barn where the yearlings were kept separate from the ewes and lambs. Steven came, too. To watch? To demand a turn working Moss? If he pestered his mother too much, she might change her mind about the whole plan.

They had to slog through the muck that surrounded the hay feeders before they reached firm ground. Janet led the way to the high end of the field.

"The dogs look like they're wearing boots," Steven said. That was true. Their white feet and legs were muddied right up to their bellies.

Janet sent Tess to gather the yearlings. Tess was slow, but she seemed to know exactly where to place herself to pull the yearlings from the feeders and bring them straight to Janet. Driving was a bit rougher. Unaccustomed to being worked, some of the yearlings resisted and tried to bolt. Janet alternated whistling and spoken commands. As far as Diane could tell, Tess obeyed either kind.

When it was Moss's turn, Janet started out whistling, then reverted to using her voice. Moss was faster than Tess, and pushier.

"What's he doing right?" Janet asked Diane. "What's he doing wrong?"

"He's . . ." Diane groped for the right word. "He's eager. That's good. But it's also maybe too much."

"Why?" Janet asked after correcting Moss and forcing him to flank wider.

"He goes too far?" Diane said.

Janet nodded. "Overflanking. And too close. So I have to back him off, slow him down, square his flanks. Like this."

She stepped forward to reinforce a command. Her even tone let Moss know he was making the correct moves. Diane tried to anticipate what Janet would say to him, but Janet was always at least two commands ahead of her.

"You try," Janet said to Diane. "Just ask him to drive the sheep straight away for a bit, nothing more."

Diane told Moss to walk up. He hesitated, glanced at Janet, then approached the sheep. They took off at a run. Now what? Diane wondered, flinging a look of panic Janet's way.

"So stop him," Janet told her quietly.

Diane yelled at Moss to lie down. Instantly he dropped to the ground. The sheep kept going.

Janet, behind her, said, "Guess you need to flank him wide, then stop him as soon as he checks them."

How to do that? Send him to the right? That would be "away to me."

By the time Diane figured out what to say, the yearlings were back at the hay feeders.

"Call him to you," Janet instructed. "Send him on an outrun."

"I take too long. I can't think what to tell him," Diane said as Moss returned to her.

"It takes practice. And, Diane, no need to yell at the dog."

"Can I try?" asked Steven. "I won't yell."

"When we get the sheep home," Janet told him. "Diane only has weekends."

Diane sent Moss for the sheep. He cast out wide, flowing away before turning in through the muck to force the sheep from the feeders. "Now what?" she said nervously.

"You don't need to tell him anything," Janet told her. "He's getting the job done. Sort of," she added, as the sheep spread out in front of Moss.

"He's too close," Diane said. "Right?"

"Right," Janet answered. "So?"

"Slow him? Make him get back? How?"

"Try a down," Janet said quietly.

"Lie down," Diane bellowed.

"Diane yelled again," Steven said.

Diane felt like strangling him. By now the sheep had split into two groups. Diane told Moss to walk up. He flanked wide to put the groups together. The sheep zigzagged up the hill. She asked him to lie down again, not yelling this time. As soon as he stopped, the sheep flowed more evenly. They flowed right past her, though, because she forgot to send him around to check them.

"Good," said Janet decisively. "There's your starting lesson. Time to let the sheep catch their breath. Tell Moss, 'That'll do,' and walk him out of here."

"Good boy," Diane murmured to the mud-spattered dog. "Thank you," she added. But she couldn't help blurting, "When you do it, when Zanna did it, it looks almost easy. I don't think I'll ever be quick enough. I'll never know what to say."

"I will," Steven volunteered.

Janet laughed. She said to Diane, "Some people never catch on. Some look as though they won't ever get it, but in time they do. At this point there's no telling, one way or the other. Zanna's a hard act to follow. Bear in mind, it didn't happen overnight for her either. And even though she was beginning to be a good novice handler, she could still blow it."

Diane didn't respond. The last thing she wanted was to give Steven another opening. But she had a sinking feeling that whatever it took to handle a sheepdog was beyond her reach.

11 Diane sat at her cousin Connie's desk and stared at the computer screen. "Janet doesn't work dogs much because she has to work at the new garden center," she typed. "She wants to grow herbs that make medicines. Rick says either herbs or dogs, not both. She might bring sheep from the farm." Diane paused, deleted the last sentence, and typed, "I asked her if I could work with Moss, and now she might bring some sheep from the farm." Diane read this over. Too much like bragging, she decided.

She restored the sentence she had deleted. Later, if she got anywhere with Moss, she would drop a casual word about working him. It was time to change the subject.

Diane had to stifle an impulse to write about her mother and Mark. Not that they had actually spelled out their plans yet. But Diane understood that something big was happening.

In the old days Diane and Zanna would have chewed over every hint that Diane picked up, inventing one scenario after another. They didn't do that anymore. Even if Diane laid out all the possibilities—from Mom's learning how to drive an eighteen-wheeler so she could hit the road with Mark to Mom's getting pregnant on purpose and starting a new family—Zanna wouldn't bother to rate them. She would probably be surprised to learn that Diane's mother was still seeing the truck driver named Mark.

Diane didn't mind about him and her mom really. But she felt closed out of their space, especially when Mom made an effort to include her. Still, that wasn't news, was it? Certainly not anything Zanna cared about.

Diane typed, "Steven wants a new name that sounds like Jace. He thinks Jace is cool, even though he's all spooked over some ghost. I've seen Fennella twice. She thinks you're the best."

"You almost through?" Connie asked. It wasn't so much a question as an order for Diane to vacate the room.

Diane sent the message. She pushed away from Connie's desk.

"How come Zanna never sends you e-mail?" Connie asked.

Diane said she didn't know. Maybe Zanna's older sister hogged the computer. Maybe Zanna was into something new and didn't care all that much about news from the other end of the country. Didn't care about her dog? Her best friend?

When Diane let Zanna know she was going to spend the summer with the Pragers, Zanna hadn't reacted much, except to warn Diane that she might get bored away from all her friends. At the time Diane had dismissed the thought. But now, with school nearly over, she wasn't so sure of what she was getting into.

The next weekend did nothing to boost her confidence. The weather was dismal, the boys got on each other's nerves, and the training session turned out to be a total bust. It wasn't just the drizzle that made Sunday morning bone-chilling. Since Gordon hadn't gotten around to moving the sheep yet, Janet took Diane and the boys and the dogs to the farm again.

Gordon, not looking all that pleased to see them, said he didn't have time to worry about sheep right now. Then he stomped off to the barn.

Dot spoke up for him. "He's worried. That heifer? She's failing, and your dad doesn't know what's wrong. For a while he guessed she'd gotten into some poisonous plant out in the woods. That could still be it. Fennella made him call Cliff Canaday, even though bringing in a vet can make matters worse. He took blood samples, but nothing turned up. He suggested another look at her, but Gordon told him to forget it. He wasn't about to put good money after bad. What really scares him is the state maybe slapping a quarantine on the herd."

"That wouldn't happen if there's no diagnosis, would it?"

Dot shrugged. "It's not knowing what's wrong with her. First she stops eating. Then she stands with her head down, drooling. Hind end's going now."

Janet frowned. "I'm really sorry, Mom. We'll go work the dogs and then get out of the way."

"You boys want to come inside with me?" Dot said.

Steven hesitated. But already his face was pinched with cold.

"Go on in with Grandma and warm up," Janet urged. "We won't be long."

Diane was elated because she wouldn't have Steven around keeping score. But right from the start Moss took it into his head to resist her. Even after she repeated commands until he finally obeyed, mostly he ended up wrong because by then the sheep had shifted. Finally Janet called a halt to the whole exercise.

"Come on," she said. "I want a look at that heifer before we pick up the boys."

"But shouldn't we end with something successful?" Diane asked.

Janet gave her a look. "Success isn't always handy by," she remarked dryly.

"Did I spoil everything because I yelled at him last time?" Diane meant: Would Moss hate her forever?

"Lighten up," Janet told her. "Constant yelling could ruin him, but not one bad working session. Sheepdogs have forgiving natures. You'll see."

"But how will he know I'm sorry?" Diane asked.

"You'll show him by not doing it anymore," Janet told her.

Diane watched Moss pick up a stick and race off with it in his mouth. Anyone who didn't know better would never have guessed that he had been less than perfect. He ran around Tess, who showed her teeth at him as she picked her way over the slimy patches. Moss just raced in wider circles, kicked up muddy water, and then dashed in close, imploring her to grab one end of his stick.

"She used to like him," Diane murmured, sad for Moss because he seemed so out of place.

"She did, and she will," Janet answered. "Only not while she has the puppies."

They crossed the dirt road. At the barn Janet made the dogs lie down on the concrete ramp before she led the way inside.

It was easy to find the affected heifer because she was all by herself in a pen. The scratches on her face were still visible, but they seemed to be healing. She looked dazed, though, stupefied. Janet turned away. "We'll hose the dogs now," she said in a hushed voice, sounding like someone at a sickbed or in a hospital.

Her father drove up with a huge round bale of hay on the

forklift. He left the tractor idling and walked over to Janet. "Well?" he said. "Did you look at her?"

Janet nodded.

"Well?" he said again.

"Not poison, I'd guess."

He looked down at his feet. Janet looked at hers. "Any others showing signs?" she asked.

He shook his head. "So far so good."

"I don't know, Dad. I just don't know."

"Join the club," he told her grimly. Then he went back to his tractor.

Janet turned on the spigot and began to uncoil the hose.

12

After their totally useless performance with the sheep, Diane was ready to give up the whole idea of working Moss. Then she figured out what had gone wrong. It was right before her eyes. Being tied all week had turned Moss sour.

She couldn't wait to get back to the Pragers, back to Moss. She would plead for his freedom, supervised freedom.

But when Friday rolled around, she had to put her campaign on hold. Walking up from the main road, she discovered two cars parked at the driveway entrance to the Pederson house. The wooded path beyond them was partly cleared. She was tempted to wait for Jace to catch up just to see his reaction. But she didn't want to delay getting to Moss. Hurrying on, she slipped her backpack from her shoulder.

At the garden center Rick was loading his truck. Toolbox in hand, he asked her to mind the place until Jace arrived.

Janet, who was off on an errand, had Tim with her. Mrs. Dworsky had met Steven at his bus stop and taken him home with her until someone was free to get him. But right now Diane was needed here.

"Will you be back soon?" she asked anxiously. What if Jace didn't come?

"In a bit," he said, slinging the toolbox into the cab and getting in beside it. "Ralph Slade's in a flap over the condition of the house. He had a guy in there with a brushhog, but he won't let him finish clearing the driveway until the house is closed off. He wants me to cover a hole or barricade the door or something so that no one can get in. He's picked the worst time, but now that you're here I can stick on a Band-Aid or two and get him off my back."

At the moment there were only two customers. Fortunately they knew exactly what they wanted, so all Diane had to do was take their money and make some change. After that she waited. What was taking Jace so long today? The minute he appeared she would go to Moss.

She filled spaces in the flats where plants had been removed, she separated the lemon thyme from the creeping thyme, and then she watered the patio tomatoes in the big pots. When Rick returned and saw what she'd done, his mood might improve. Enough for her to speak out about Moss? She'd have to wait and see.

After a while a car pulled into the parking area. Jace came biking right behind it. A woman got out of the car. "I hope you're Jace," she said. "Mr. Prager needs a six-foot length of irrigation pipe. He says you know where to find it. If you're quick, I'll give you a lift. Not into that driveway, though." She touched her front fender. "I'm not scratching any more paint."

Jace said, "Irrigation pipe? What for?"

"I was there to take pictures," she told him. "You know where it is? I've got to get going."

Jace nodded. He walked his bike around to the rear of the garden center and reappeared with a section of pipe. He sent a questioning glance at Diane. "Something going on over there?"

The woman said, "The owner wants to keep out . . . I don't know what. I mean, does he really need that pile of junk to discourage visitors? Only dumb animals would go into a place like that, and they won't sue him."

"You saw . . . something?" Jace asked her.

"More than I bargained for," she declared. "You coming or not? Can you stick that thing out the window? Careful." She grabbed a camera and placed it in front.

Diane took pity on him. "Hey, Jace," she said, "you know more about plants than I do. Why don't you stay here for the customers and let me take the pipe?"

He reddened. "Is that okay?" he asked the woman.

"How do I know?" she replied. "The man just said irrigation pipe."

So Diane got in back for the short ride down the hill. When the car stopped, the woman kept saying, "Careful!" as Diane pulled the pipe through the window. It was heavier than she expected, so she drew it hand over hand to ease the end out and down without scraping more paint. The car lurched off.

Diane dragged the pipe past Rick's truck and the other car. Beyond them the ground was torn and littered, but she had no trouble until she came to what looked like a mountain of brush and rubble. How was she supposed to get around it? She broke through dead blackberry canes that snagged her jeans and shirt. She heard hammering. That sounded promising. The sweet fragrance of apple blossoms beckoned. But all she could see ahead were parts of a wheelbarrow, a rusted bedspring, and window frames with shards of glass hanging loose.

She called to Rick, and he answered.

"I have the pipe. How do I get there?"

"Hold on," he told her. "It's our baby-sitter," he said to someone else. "Can you get the pipe from her?"

A moment later a man crashed through the debris. "Some mess, huh?" he said as he reached for the pipe. "Next time try the other way around."

Diane made her way back to the road. Stopping at the garden center, she found Jace finishing with another customer.

"You okay?" she asked.

"How about you?" he returned. "You heard the lady. She saw."

Diane started to contradict him, then thought better of it and went straight to Moss. He wouldn't even raise his head from the ground. Still, she sat there beside him until Janet returned with the boys.

Diane got through the rest of the afternoon playing with the puppies and letting Steven show her what he was teaching the lambs. After the animals had been fed, she cooked up some gluey macaroni and cheese and gave the boys an early supper. They were watching a children's program when Rick and Janet came in talking about what they could do for Ralph Slade.

"He says landscaping, but I've a feeling what he wants is a caretaker," Rick said. "I don't know what to charge. And how can I take time off our own business?"

Janet said, "Isn't it sort of an extension of our business?"

"I don't know." Rick rubbed his forehead. "Is it?"

They ate in silence for a few minutes. Then Rick spoke again. "If it is, where does it leave your medicinal herbs?"

Janet said, "I'll barely get started this year, especially if I take time for dog trialing." She looked at Diane. "Everyone needs to do something they love."

Now was the time to speak up. Diane drew a big breath and declared, "Moss will never be any good if he's depressed and frustrated. Doesn't he deserve another chance?"

"Lots of working dogs are tied," Janet told her. "Often for their own safety. They're none the worse for it. I know Moss acts like he's being punished, but he's not."

Stalling, Diane said, "I forgot. I made a salad." She brought it to the table. She understood that freedom alone wasn't enough to turn Moss into a happy dog. Yet she believed it was where to begin. "I'll work with him," she promised. "He's no more harmful than your next-door ghost. Anyway, he's a lot nicer, if you listen to Jace. What's wrong with a friendly dog that most of your customers like?"

Laughing, Rick said he wasn't responsible for the Pederson ghost. But Janet sided with Diane. Their business wasn't going to fail because Moss got into a customer's car.

Rick rubbed his whole head. "All right," he finally agreed. "Only think of it this way. He's on probation. You understand?"

Diane sighed. Now she would have to find a way to turn Moss around.

Her resolve sustained her through the next weekend, which she spent at home so that her mother could do some clothes shopping with her and sort through Connie's discarded things. Her mother was being extra-nice and generous, especially since all Diane really needed over the summer were jeans and shorts and T-shirts and maybe a couple of sweatshirts. Mom even sprang for Diane's birthday present of Legos for Steven.

On Saturday Mom and Mark took her out for a spaghetti dinner, and Mark said that from now on they ought to make a regular habit of a night out like that, say, once a month.

Diane braced herself for the big announcement that seemed to lurk behind this cozy future he pictured. Were they getting married? Were they planning to start a new family? What if Mom was secretly counting on all of Diane's time with the Pragers to lay the groundwork for endless baby-sitting?

Diane told them about Steven's wanting to change his name to Mace. They laughed at that. They laughed a lot that evening, and Diane laughed with them. Then, on the way home, she was suddenly carsick. Mark had to pull over quickly to let her out. Too much spaghetti, Mom said. Diane shook her head. Too much laughing, she thought. Something like that. Wondering if they were disgusted with her. Fed up.

Afterward she thought about going to bed every single night in the Pragers' house. Sleeping on the living-room couch was fine for a weekend, but it might not be so great if she felt crummy the way she had this evening.

Actually she didn't feel so bad anymore, now that she

was in her own bed. Forget the dark. She was enclosed by walls and things so familiar that she could pin a donkey's tail on any object: windowsill, mirror, even that goofy photo taken at last year's fair showing Zanna and her sitting side by side like dolls in a giant chair.

For a while she listened through her closed door to television voices and tried to identify the program. Were Mom and Mark engrossed in what they were watching? If they were using the tube to cover their own conversation, they might be talking about their plans, about Diane.

The background music changed; the television voices suddenly louder, more strident. Probably a commercial. Sighing, Diane rolled over and burrowed down under the covers.

Sunday morning she sent another e-mail to Zanna and then waited and waited for a reply.

"Don't forget the time difference," Connie told her.

Diane had forgotten. Besides, it was impossible to guess what life was like out there in California.

At noon she sent another message, one designed to prod Zanna into responding. "I've started working Moss," Diane wrote. "He's kind of rusty so far. Hope to get him ready for a trial soon."

She waited some more. Then Connie said, "Face it, Diane, your friend doesn't check e-mail every day. And I need to use the computer."

So Diane went home.

"Can I call Zanna?" she asked her mother.

"Call? On the telephone? I thought you just e-mailed her."

"I did. She didn't get it. Can I, please?"

Mark said, "Why not? It can't cost that much on Sunday if she sticks to five minutes."

Zanna's sister answered the phone, then yelled for Zanna.

"I e-mailed you," Diane said. "Don't you ever check for messages?"

"Not all the time," Zanna answered. "How's Moss?"

"Good. Fine. We're bringing sheep from the farm, and I've started to work him."

"Oh," said Zanna.

"Janet doesn't have much time this year. She hasn't gone to any sheepdog trials yet. They're keeping a puppy, though. He's sort of for the boys, but Janet will train him. You wouldn't believe—"

Mom said, "Finish up, Diane."

It couldn't be five minutes yet.

"When do you think you'll get back to Maine?" Diane asked Zanna.

"I don't know." Zanna sounded so distant. "It costs too much to fly, and we're going to a ranch this summer for two weeks. I'm going to ride horseback every day."

A ranch. Horses. Was this Zanna's new life? Diane reminded Zanna to check her e-mail if she wanted updates on Moss's progress. The conversation was over.

 Maybe it was just wishful thinking, but it seemed to Diane that Moss greeted her with fresh enthusiasm. Because she hadn't seen him for two weeks? Because Mom drove her out to Janet's, meaning that Diane was delivered to him from a newly arrived car? Or because he had begun to feel attached to her?

The boys were excited, too. They acted as though Diane had been away for ages. They couldn't wait to show her the small upstairs storage room that had been cleared out for her to sleep in. Did she know that all the puppies had gone to their new homes, except for Tad, who was staying? Did she realize that she had missed Steven's birthday and that he had lost a tooth the very same day? Had she heard about the lambs getting out again and being gone overnight without being eaten by coyotes? Could she guess where she was to keep her clothes? Was she informed about their summer bedtime? It stayed light much later now. Had she noticed how light it was?

The questions tumbled out of them while the puppy hurled itself onto her mattress bed, grabbed a corner of the pillow, and began to drag it onto the floor. Mom was downstairs talking with Janet. Moss stood in the doorway, his eyes on all of them, growling softly when Tad charged over to him. Tad dropped to his belly and groveled under Moss's head.

Diane was supposed to unpack right away because Mom had to take the suitcase back with her. Janet had supplied the flats they used for small plants. They could be stacked like drawers. Diane could have as many as she needed.

She eyed the puppy. "Tad can't come in when no one's here," she told the boys. "That's a rule."

Steven said, "He's not very good about rules yet."

"A rule for you guys," she said. "Anyway, he's your puppy, isn't he?"

"Yes," said Steven. "Because I can't have Moss. He's partly for my birthday."

"He's mine, too," Tim said.

"We have to share," Steven explained, "but Tim's too little to train him."

"I am not." Tim's voice rose. "Tad's my best friend."

Diane shoved the puppy and the boys out of the little room and heard them clatter down the stairs. With the door closed, and with no window, it felt like being in a closet. But having this private space was what counted. She dumped out the suitcase onto the mattress. She could stow things away later on.

When she opened the door, Moss was waiting for her. Kneeling beside him, she gave him a hug and whispered, "You're allowed in here. Want to see?" She let him inside. Moss stood beside the mattress bed, his tail waving slowly. Shoving her clothes to one side, she made a space for him. He stepped onto the bed and sat down. She said, "That's right. This is where you belong."

But as soon as she picked up the suitcase, he bounded ahead of her and downstairs to the kitchen full of mothers and boys and puppy.

Tim, who had been telling Diane's mom about the room they'd fixed up, asked her if she was going upstairs to see it.

She glanced at her watch before answering. "Sure," she told him. "It's really nice of all of you to make Diane so welcome."

Thinking of the dumped clothes and the plastic trays, Diane said, "Not now." Mom wouldn't think that tiny, windowless room was so cool. If she spoke her mind, it would be worse than embarrassing. "Next time, when you visit," Diane told her. "I haven't put anything away yet. It's a mess."

Mom laughed. "Like I've never seen a mess before?" Still, she picked up the empty suitcase and moved toward the door. Turning, she opened her arms for Diane and held her a moment. "Have fun," she whispered. "Be good."

Later, after Diane's mother had driven away, Janet went to the garden center for a while, and the boys took over.

"At the farm Grandpa dug a big hole," Tim told her. "He buried a cow in it, and the legs stuck up."

"It was gross," Steven said. "Tim likes gross stuff."

"I do not," Tim protested. "I don't talk about ghosts either. You're the one that does."

Steven said, "Well, Jace, he's been to the haunted house. And Great-Grandma Fennella says that a man really did live in it for years and years without coming out. His brother brought him cookies and stuff. Jace says that when the house gets knocked down, everyone will find out what's inside."

"Tad!" shouted Tim as a puddle spread beneath the puppy.

"You're not supposed to yell at him," Steven said. Swooping down to pick up the puppy, he carried him, still dribbling, to the back door.

"Well, he's not supposed to pee on the floor," Tim retorted.

"He'll learn," Diane said as she wiped up the puddle and the wet trail to the door. "He can't always remember to ask to go outside yet."

"Like you in diapers," Steven told Tim.

"I'm not in diapers," Tim declared. "They're Pull-Ups, and only sometimes at night when I'm sleeping."

Diane glared at Steven. "It's an in-between time," she said. "Everyone goes through it."

"Everyone?" asked Tim.

"Everyone!" she asserted. "It's part of growing up."

"And growing down, too," said Steven. "Great-Grandpa Rob wore diapers. I saw them. And sometimes he peed into a bottle."

Diane wasn't sure where to take this subject. Should she try to explain that the boys' great-grandfather had been paralyzed? Better not, she decided. That was up to Janet.

Diane was on firmer ground debunking ghosts and their like. And someday, maybe soon, she would set Jace straight about scaring younger kids. As if there wasn't enough of that sort of thing on the tube to give them nightmares.

 Diane discovered the advantage of the later bedtime for the boys. They were still asleep when she and Janet took the dogs out to the yearlings for an early lesson in the pale morning mist.

When Janet worked Moss, it always looked so simple and straightforward that Diane couldn't tell where she herself went wrong. When she tried to work him, everything happened so fast that even when she managed to think of the right command, by the time she said it, a different one was needed.

Sometimes Janet let the puppy tag along with them to the field. Usually he ran around on his own or followed whichever dog was working. But once in a while he focused on the sheep, and then his whole manner changed. For a moment or so he became a tiny sheepdog, intent on herding. Mostly he ended up scattering the sheep or simply getting distracted and chasing after a bird or a squirrel. Janet would continue working Tess or Moss right through this upheaval without ever raising her voice or losing track of what she was doing.

"Don't be so impatient," she told Diane. "It takes lots of

practice. You need to understand the animals you're herd-ing, not just the dogs."

"We got those heifers back, though," Diane said, "and I don't know anything about cows."

"You were lucky," Janet told her. "Moss was doing it on his own for you. He started out as a cattle dog. Before Zanna came on the scene, before my grandfather had his stroke, when Moss was just a promising young sheepdog, he was already working the cows. He'll never lose what he learned back then."

Moss, waiting for the next command, held the sheep in a tight cluster. It was obvious that he knew when Janet was speaking to him and when she wasn't. Everything seemed suspended, the day holding its breath for this one instant. Then Janet said, "That'll do, Moss." The dog turned away from the sheep. They stood for a moment longer, not quite sure they had been released. Then, leaping high in the sud-den rush of freedom, they bolted.

For Diane the early-morning sessions always seemed too short. She kept thinking she was just about to get her com-mands and timing right. Or was she kidding herself?

In exchange for these lessons, she was expected to help in the gardens as well as to keep the boys out of the garden center, to clean up the kitchen after breakfast and lunch, to watch out for the puppy, and to check up on Steven's care of the lambs, which he had named Aster and Nutmeg. All this made for a full day.

While she was getting used to the routine, she collapsed at night, too tired to read or even to watch television. Moss always sensed when she was conking out. Without being called, he would appear at her door, nose it open, and creep across her discarded clothes to stretch out beside her on the mattress. But it was too close in the airless room. After a few minutes he would slide onto the floor, and in the morning she would find him there, lying on his back with his legs splayed out.

One afternoon during that first full week, the puppy disappeared. Diane and the boys went calling everywhere. When Diane's urgency made Tess uneasy and she crept away to the shade of the barn, Diane turned to Moss.

"Find Tad," she told him. "Find the tadpole."

Moss waved his tail at her.

"Look!" she commanded. She dragged the puppy's bed out onto the porch. "Look!" she repeated.

Moss did look, but without taking a step.

"He thinks you mean sheep," Steven said.

"Moss, look!" She called the puppy in the high-pitched voice they used to get him to come. Then she repeated the command: "Moss, look!"

Off he went, sniffing the ground, circling and circling.

"I'm telling Mom," Steven said.

"Not yet," Diane told him. "Wait a minute."

"Tad might be in trouble," Steven insisted.

"What kind of trouble?" Tim demanded.

Steven said, "He could be trapped. Or stolen."

"Stolen?" wailed Tim.

"Steven!" Diane snapped. "That's not helping. Just lay off."

Even though Moss kept doubling back, the trail he seemed to be following past the gardens led toward the woods. By now Tim was crying and shouting at Diane to wait for him. "Stay with your brother," she told Steven. "Please," she added.

"You're not supposed to leave us," he said.

She didn't know what to do. Of course, he was right, but she was afraid of losing track of Moss.

Just then Jace came trudging up the driveway from the garden center. "Jace," she shouted, "watch the boys."

"Can't," he called back. "I've just come to get a rope."

"Please," she pleaded. "You have to." She plunged after Moss, following the sounds he made since he was already lost to sight. She picked her way through brush and around blowdowns on land Janet and Rick intended to clear eventually to expand their nursery. As she stumbled along, from time to time she called the puppy.

Then suddenly she nearly fell over Moss, who had stopped short, allowing the whimpering but ecstatic Tad to crawl between his legs.

"Tad! Good boy. Look," she told Moss, "you found him. You're the best. Did you know that?"

Moss drew back from the wriggling pup and uttered a low warning growl, as if to let Tad know that enough was enough.

Diane looked around. What had kept the puppy from returning on his own? He must have lost his sense of direction and continued straight on until her calling or Moss on his track got through to him. She was still puzzling over this as she carried Tad home. What mattered, she decided, was that the puppy was safe and that Moss had understood her, even if what she asked of him had nothing to do with sheepherding.

Tim was overjoyed. Steven told her to make sure Tad wasn't injured.

"He looks scared," Jace said. "He was heading for the Pederson place. Maybe he saw old Axel's ghost. They say animals can see things we can't see."

"There isn't any ghost," Diane retorted.

"All that commotion can shake a ghost loose," Steven explained. He turned to Jace. "Right? Isn't that what your grandfather told you?"

Diane sent Jace a look. Why couldn't he keep his worries to himself? "Thanks," she said. She could tell from his answering nod that her sarcasm had escaped him.

"Anyway," said Tim, his arms clasped tightly around the errant puppy, "Tad didn't get stolen."

"Or hurt," Diane added. "Let's get him inside now. I don't want to have to think about him for a while." She glanced over at Moss, who had settled himself on the porch. "And thanks to you, too," she murmured lovingly as she carried Tad past him into the house.

 By the time the garden center closed, the puppy incident was old news.

"*I* wanted to tell you," Steven said.

"Well, Jace already did," Rick told him. "You're going to have to keep a sharper eye out from now on."

"Nothing bad happened," Steven said.

"Did you water the lambs?" asked Janet, on her way out to the barn.

"Everything's done, even the chickens." Steven replied. "Diane helped."

"Good," said Rick. "Now listen, boys." He emptied out a bag of salad greens into a wooden bowl. "I don't want to scare you, but there's a good reason why I don't want you going through the woods beyond our property."

Janet came back inside in time to hear these last few

words. She said, "You always played in the woods when you were a kid. I think you ought to explain what we're concerned about."

Rick nodded. "Right. Well, it's the old Pederson place. It's a mess. Much worse than when I used to go there years ago. The house is so dilapidated that anyone could get hurt in it. So don't go near there, even if you hear people working."

"We didn't," Steven protested.

Tim said. "Anyway, we already know it's a bad place. It's hunted."

"Haunted," Steven corrected.

Their father dumped leftover stew into a pan. "That's what kids say to scare each other," he told them. "And I'm asking you two boys to be just a little bit scared, or careful, that's all."

"Because there really is a ghost, like Jace says?" asked Steven.

"No. Listen." Rick turned from the stove. "Jace is—" He flung Janet a look.

"Jace is kind of exaggerating." Janet explained for him. "People do that sometimes when they tell stories. It doesn't make them liars."

"And when people are nervous or frightened, they can go overboard," Rick added.

"How? What do they do?" Steven asked him.

Rick thought for a minute. Then he said, "Well, look at how some people kill every snake they come across. They don't stop to figure out what kind of snake it is. The sight of a snake scares the daylights out of people like that, so they just bash it."

"Jace doesn't do that," Steven said. "Anyhow, you can't kill a ghost."

Rick laughed. "Good point, Steven. You're right. Jace is no way that bad about his ghost. I used an extreme example to show you what unchecked fear can lead to. That's why it's important to make sense of scary things before they take over. That's all I was trying to say."

At supper Rick and Janet rehashed garden center plans.

"Think you can back off the sheepdog trials this summer?" Rick asked her.

Diane froze. If Janet gave up trialing, where would that leave Moss?

"I haven't been to a trial this season," Janet said. "Yet," she added.

"Exactly," said Rick. "And we're already spread too thin."

"You keep saying 'we,' but you mean 'me.'"

Rick sighed. "I mean both of us. Everything."

"Who's too thin?" asked Steven.

"That means having too many things to do," Rick told him.

"I'm going to only a few trials this season," Janet said. "And you'll have Jace here those weekends."

Diane resumed eating. She didn't dare look at Janet or Rick.

"Jace is no substitute for you," Rick told her.

Janet laughed. "I'm glad you think so. Seriously, though, a few trials won't amount to much. Diane and the boys will be with me. You and Jace can manage."

Rick pushed back his chair. "You know what I'm looking forward to?" he asked.

"What?" said Janet.

"I'm looking forward to a time when we aren't flat out every minute of every day."

"I know," Janet replied, beginning to gather the plates.

Diane offered to clean up, but Janet declined. "Go out with the boys."

"Let's teach Tad to bring the ball," Tim said as he ran to the door.

Outside Steven asked her, "Why do grown-ups say things like 'too thin' and 'flat out' if they mean something else? And how come nothing's ever too fat or too thick?"

Diane shrugged and then laughed. "Beats me," she told him.

"Beat you?" he exclaimed, charging her and trying to drag her down.

"That's not what I meant," she shouted, running and catching up to Tim. "Save me," she cried, dodging around the smaller boy. "Your brother's gone mad."

"Mad!" roared Steven, snarling fiercely at Tim. "I'm a mad dog."

"Don't," Diane said to Steven. "That's the kind of stuff Jace does."

Steven drew up. "Okay, Tim, I'm not mad anymore. I just got cured."

Tim regarded him warily. "Mad dogs are on TV," he said. "Right?"

"Right," Diane told him. "On stupid horror shows." Like ghosts, she almost added. "Now where's that ball for Tad?"

 Moss was ready for the first sheepdog trial. Diane wasn't.

Janet said so straight out. "Maybe later in the summer," she said. "Or maybe there'll be a trial with a youth class."

"What about me?" Steven demanded. "I'm the real kid here."

Janet said, "You've got years left to be one, too, and do trials. Let's give Diane a chance if one comes her way."

Diane understood what Janet implied. No point throwing away an opportunity for Moss to compete. She tried not to mind. After all, she was still working with him. At least she hadn't spoiled him for Janet to run.

They left before sunup, and the boys slept most of the way. When they arrived at the trial field, Tess and Moss stood up, woke the boys, and set a tone of anticipation that reminded Diane of last year.

But that brought back dreaded memories as well. Diane would never forget the thrill of sending Moss out for sheep that had been chased away by coyotes. Other dogs had been sent as well, so she'd known that was the thing to do. Moss, already stirred up, had taken off like a shot. Most of the dogs had returned, a few torn up by the coyotes. But not Moss. He had vanished. Forever, Janet had finally come to believe. Until, months later, he had turned up in the midst of another sheepdog trial.

Diane's face burned as the fear and guilt came rushing back. Not even the amazing relief of his return could erase the misery she had lived through. Was that part of why she could never quite take hold when she worked him now?

Everyone greeting Janet wanted to know why she had missed the earlier trials. Some of them nodded at Diane, who smiled back even though she couldn't remember most of their names. She looked around for kids who might occupy the boys, so that she would be free to watch the dogs. She wantcd to study them. She was determined to learn from them.

The trial course was laid out on a green hillside with mountains beyond. The white gates through which the sheep were to be fetched or driven must have been freshly painted. Even the sheep looked uniform, all of one breed and size. And there were several sets of bleachers for the audience, which was already beginning to arrive. Diane had been to enough trials to realize that this one was a notch above the usual farm event. No wonder Janet had been firm about running Moss herself. Diane wouldn't have dared set foot on that course.

The first thing the boys did was to run to the handlers' tent to check for free doughnuts beside the coffeepot. Within minutes other kids were flocking to the snack table. Diane hung around until Steven and Tim connected with these kids and they took over the nearest bleacher. Soon the older ones were using the upper benches as parallel bars and balance beams while Tim's group at the lower levels practiced jumping to the ground.

At least for a while Diane was free. She checked the big board to see where Tess and Moss placed in the running order. Tess was sixteenth. Moss was forty-fourth. Diane tried to calculate what time that might be. At the rate of six or seven runs an hour, Moss wouldn't get out on the course until midafternoon.

Each run began when the handler cast off the dog for the long outrun up the hill. The handler lost points if she whistled or called to the dog before the outrun was completed as the dog came around behind the sheep. Diane found that she could see what Janet always maintained: that this first phase of work determined much of the rest of the run. Pushy dogs moved the sheep too fast, and fast sheep tended to excite those dogs and make them even pushier. But control by itself wasn't the name of the game either. Some dogs were so overcommanded that they couldn't use their natural abilities to advantage.

When Janet and Tess walked to the post, Diane found herself clutching the fence so hard that the wire bit into her palms. She couldn't imagine standing at the post and working a dog at such a distance. Did Janet ever feel like quitting before she started?

"Tim has to go to the toilet," Steven said behind her.

"Tell him to wait," said Diane.

"He has to go."

Diane groaned. Right then and there she vowed never, ever would she be saddled with kids of her own like these. But the moment after she had hoisted Tim onto the high seat in the porta-potty and he clutched her for fear of falling in, she felt her heart soften. Maybe a kid like him wouldn't be so terrible, she decided as he ran back to join the cluster of children now playing underneath the bleacher.

Janet said Tess had been a bit slow, as was to be expected so soon after her pups, but there had been no major faults. Tess, still panting, lay on her side next to the water bowl. Moss, at the end of his chain, set his pleading gaze on Janet, who suggested that Diane take him for a walk away from the trial field.

"Down," Diane ordered as his forefeet lifted in small leaps of joy. She glanced around to be sure that no critical eye observed his goofy prancing. Then she gave up the pretense of being a handler with a serious dog and started running with him past the parked cars and into the woodlot beyond.

When she unhooked his leash, he paused, his ears erect, his body poised for action. "That'll do," she told him. "That'll do, Moss."

He charged up the path while she jogged along, willing herself not to nag him. Suddenly doubling back, he raced past her and turned sharply to investigate something in the undergrowth. She kept going. In a moment he would be with her again. But when the moment passed, she had to stop, in the grip of panic. Shouting for him, she tore back, her breath short and hard, her next call a scream.

He appeared farther along the path. He looked as if he had already started back without her to find Janet or the van.

"Moss!" she called hoarsely, dropping to her knees. He trotted toward her, slowing as he approached. "Moss, here!" she ordered, her voice choked with anger. Moss lowered his head and crept to her.

"Moss," she said, her anger dissolving into shame over losing control of herself and blaming him. It was her doing, her fault, not his. "I'm sorry," she whispered, hugging him to her. Although he wouldn't raise his head, he submitted to her embrace. Then, after a moment, she felt him give in some more as he leaned against her.

If only she could unburden the past like this. But how could Moss forgive her for failing him that first time, the time when he was lost for so long and injured so badly, if he didn't connect her with it?

"Moss," she repeated, and up came his muzzle, thrust into the crook of her arm, as close as he could be.

At first the boys squabbled over the ribbon Moss won until Janet told them that if they couldn't share it, she'd take it back. Diane thought that if she had run Moss and had come in eighth out of sixty-five dogs, she would hang the ribbon in her room. But Janet cared more about the check handed out with the ribbon.

The ride home was satisfying because the boys, who had played hard all day, finished a bag of popcorn and then drowsed in the backseat. That allowed Janet to talk about the runs and to explain some of the finer points to Diane. And to go over Moss's run yet again.

Diane had overlooked small deviations from what seemed to her an otherwise perfect run. She blamed the sheep for resisting Moss. If he had run earlier when they were fresh, they would have moved more freely.

Janet said, "A good dog meets every condition. One ornery ewe can spoil an entire run. The heat of the day can affect sheep and dogs. Or wind can stir them up. Moss did well enough. Most of the dogs competing today have been trialing since the end of April. It may take one or two more trials before Moss goes to the post entirely focused and takes everything in stride."

"And you?" Diane asked. "Do you take it in stride?"

Janet sent her a swift glance, then smiled. "Good question. I suppose I'm pretty realistic about our chances. I don't get too excited when I win, so why should I get all bummed out when I don't?"

Diane sighed. She said, "I could never be that—that—" She didn't know how to finish.

"You think it's cool to be so levelheaded," Janet told her. "But there was a time when I longed to win. And hated to losc." She paused. "Trialing wasn't much fun then." She went on to talk about one of the dogs today that had had a beautiful run until, at the very end, it had taken a swipe at a sheep and been disqualified. "Too much pressure on that dog. The dogs should love working sheep anywhere and everywhere. Not just to please me."

Diane said, "That time with Fennella when Moss brought the heifers back. That was the greatest."

Janet slowed and pulled into a gas station. Before getting out, she said, "That's where it really counts, too. Remember, there are good dogs and good handlers who never make it on the trial scene. But you could learn more watching them herd stock in a real-life situation than at most events like today's trial."

Stopping roused the boys, so Diane took them to the toilet while Janet pumped gas. Back in the van again the boys were wide-awake. That ended the dog talk. But they were almost home now. Janet assigned each of them a job to do before supper.

Tim said, "I can do something outside, too."

"Setting the table will be a big help," Janet replied. "And if you want, you can feed the dogs."

"I'll need a flashlight," Steven said importantly.

Diane hoped Janet would tell him there was no need to make a big deal about feeding the lambs. It only made Tim envious.

When they tumbled out of the van, each of them headed off in a different direction. Diane went straight to the puppy, who had spent a long, lonely day confined in his pen. After cleaning up his messes, she tried to make him follow her to the house. But either he suspected a trap and further confinement, or else he was just too full of himself.

First he ran circles around her; then he chased after Tess, who was rolling in the driveway.

With one eye on him, Diane called Tim to come help. But Steven appeared first.

Ignoring Tad, he said, "There's something strange with Aster and Nutmeg."

"Something wrong with them?" Diane asked.

"No, they're fine. I fed them. But there's some animal with them. I didn't bring a flashlight, so I'm not sure, but I think it's dead."

Diane left Tad romping near Tess. Like the puppy, the lambs had been left in their nighttime enclosure for this long day. They looked up from their feeder when Diane and Steven came through the gate, saw no new bucket of pellets, and went back to eating.

"Over there." Tim pointed to the coiled hose. "I saw it when I filled the water tub."

In the bright moonlight the creature's close shadow gave the impression of a dog almost the size of Tess. But as Diane drew closer, she saw that it was a cat lying on its side, its legs outstretched as if it had been flung on the ground in mid-flight. Her first thought was that it was the cat that had been dumped on the road. She couldn't be sure, though. Peering down at it, what she noticed was its filthy open mouth, its lifeless eyes like black holes.

"You'd better get your mother," she told Steven.

While she waited for Janet, Diane approached the lambs. They went on calmly eating. Whatever had terrorized the cat and caused its death didn't seem to have disturbed them, at least not for long, and they appeared unharmed.

She was back for a second look at the cat when Janet

and Steven arrived. Janet raised a warning arm to keep Steven back.

"Wait," she said.

"I just want to see," he told her.

Shaking her head, she crouched down for a close look.

"What are you going to do with it?" Steven asked her. "Bury it in the manure pile with the dead hens?"

Janet rose to her feet. "Did either of you touch it?" she asked. When they shook their heads, she continued. "What about the lambs?"

"I fed them," Steven said.

"They look fine," Diane told her.

"No," Janet said sharply. "Did you touch them?"

Diane said she hadn't. Steven said he guessed not.

"But they really aren't hurt or scared or anything," Diane insisted.

"Okay," Janet said. "I want you both out of here. Now, tomorrow, and until I say you can come back in." She headed for the house.

"What about feed and water?" Steven demanded. "They're my fair project. Anyway, it can't be their fault the cat died here."

Janet told Diane to give the boys supper and get them to bed. She told Rick she needed to speak with him. They went out onto the porch.

"Where's Mom and Dad going?" Tim wanted to know. "I set the table for all of us."

"That's great," Diane told him. "They'll sit down at their places later. Right now they want you to eat something and jump into bed."

"Guess what I found?" Steven started to tell Tim.

"Not now," Diane said to him. "Let's just get some supper into you two before you're sent upstairs."

"I'm not even hungry," Tim declared. "I'm full of popcorn."

Diane glanced toward the door. She guessed that Janet and Rick were waiting for the boys to be out of the kitchen before they came back in. "Tell you what," she said. "If you get ready for bed right now, I'll bring up a peanut butter and grape jelly sandwich and a glass of milk, and you can have it in your room like a picnic."

"Me, too?" asked Steven.

She nodded. "But you have to be quick. And don't forget to wash and brush your teeth." As she slapped the sandwiches together, it occurred to her that it was pointless for them to brush their teeth if they were going to eat peanut butter afterward. Never mind, she told herself. They could make up for it in the morning.

 By the time Diane came downstairs, Janet was just hanging up the telephone. She said to Rick, "Cliff thinks it's peculiar. That's what he said: peculiar." She turned to Diane. "The vet wants the cat examined, just to be on the safe side."

The safe side of what? Diane wondered.

Rick said, "All afternoon I kept thinking I should check the animals."

"It's not your fault," Janet said. "We left it that you wouldn't have to do anything. Anyway, even if you'd looked in on the lambs, what then? The cat might've come afterward."

"It could be the one I saw thrown out of a car."

"Diane!" Janet exclaimed. "You never mentioned that."

"It was weeks ago. The cat ran into the woods. I think it was going to have kittens. But what difference would it make if I'd told you?"

"None." Janet shook her head. "None at all. Of course."

"What about the cat?" Diane asked her.

"Well, there's a chance, just a chance, mind you, that she might've been sick."

"You mean when I saw her? If it's even the same cat."

"No," Janet replied. "Sick now."

Rick said bluntly, "Janet's worried about rabies."

"Oh," said Diane. But what flashed into her mind wasn't the cat but the frenzied skunk on the road. Then she continued. "Is that why you didn't want us to touch it?"

Janet nodded.

But she hadn't wanted them to touch the lambs either, and the lambs were perfectly healthy. Was Janet making a big deal over nothing? It certainly looked that way as she inserted one plastic bag inside another, pulled on rubber gloves, and set out with Rick, who carried the big lantern and detoured to the barn for a shovel.

When they returned, they were discussing whether to store the plastic-wrapped cat overnight. Since it was supposed to be refrigerated, Rick decided to take it over to the animal clinic at once. Janet offered to, but Rick insisted. "You're beat," he said. "Eat something. Take a shower. I'll be back in twenty minutes."

Janet and Diane sat at the kitchen table and ate chicken salad.

"So how long will it take to find out about the cat?" Diane finally asked.

"Not long once the lab gets it." Abruptly Janet shoved back her chair. "I don't want to wait even that long," she declared, reaching for the phone and placing a call. "Hi, Mom," she said. "Can I speak to Dad?"

There was a considerable pause before she continued. "Dad, that heifer, the one that died? Were tissue samples taken? I know there were blood tests." Diane could hear Gordon's voice exclaiming. "Well, like the brain," Janet continued. "No, Dad, I'm not thinking about mad cow disease, and I am being serious. What about rabies?" She sat with the telephone at her ear while she stabbed a fork at a bit of celery on her plate. "Well, we found a dead cat here that's going to be tested. . . . You bet I'll let you know. . . . Right. Probably nothing. Still . . . Okay."

"If it is rabies," Diane asked after Janet hung up, "then what?"

"Then . . . I'm not sure. We might have to quarantine the lambs. The dogs are vaccinated, of course. I'm just going to have to be absolutely sure that Steven didn't come in contact with the virus. I don't want to alarm him. But if the cat tests positive, we'll need to cover that question pretty thoroughly. Anyway," she added, "there's nothing to do now. We don't need to borrow trouble. And, Diane, you were right to send Steven for me right away. Thanks."

Diane was already undressed when she thought about the skunk again. Was there a connection with the cat? How could there be? Even if the skunk had been rabid, it hadn't bitten the cat. Diane had been watching from the time the cat had been dumped till the skunk had been run over. Not that it could make any difference now. Either the cat had died of rabies or it hadn't.

Moss pushed open the door and flopped down beside her. "You're safe," she murmured. Thank goodness for that vaccination. Still, she mused, reaching over to place a hand on his head, someone, maybe the vet, might be interested in what she had seen on the road all those weeks ago.

Janet and Rick said almost nothing to Steven about the rabies possibility.

"No point blowing this out of proportion," Rick told Diane and Jace when the boys were out of earshot.

"It would be bad for business," Jace said.

"It would be bad for the kids," Rick countered.

"Let's wait for the results," Janet said. "If they're positive, then the kids will be told. I'd like Steven to learn about it from someone like Cliff who knows what he's talking about and can answer questions. Meanwhile I'm the only one who goes in with the lambs. According to Cliff, if they got bitten or scratched and a rabid animal's saliva got into their system, they'd be incubating the virus. It takes time for the disease to develop and be transmitted. But why take chances?"

"Why don't you vaccinate sheep and cows?" Diane asked.

"That's Fennella's department," Janet answered. "And Dad's."

Rick raised a warning hand as the boys and puppy came charging up to them. All at once they were discussing where to transplant Janet's medicinal herb seedlings. "Boneset and mugwort need plenty of moisture," Janet remarked. "Do you think it would help to set them close to the plants that hold dew? Coneflowers, for instance."

"We can try that," Rick replied. "The leaves of ladies' mantle might be effective, too. But sooner or later you'll need a wetland site."

"That means two new gardens!" Jace exclaimed. "I'm not digging up rocks all by myself."

"We'll start small," Janet told him. "We'll plow and harrow a little at a time."

They were still talking about soil preparation as they strode across to the garden center.

Diane could tell that the boys hadn't caught the slightest whiff of adult worry. Some parents were skilled at masking concerns. Not like Mom and Mark, who had treated Diane like visiting royalty that last weekend home. They were so attentive that she had ended up feeling like a visitor from outer space.

The day proceeded like any other, except that the air was hot and still, a haze rising to the far horizon. In the afternoon Mrs. Dworsky invited the boys up the hill for a swim with her grandchildren. Tim was recovering from yesterday's activities at the trial and wanted to stay home. Since Diane couldn't leave him alone in the house, Steven bribed him to go along with them. But Tim dragged his feet. By the time they had trudged the steep quarter mile, all he wanted to do was sit in the shade on the grassy bank while Steven and a few other kids splashed and swam and tried to duck one another.

"None of that," Mrs. Dworsky told them.

"We're just fooling around," one kid explained.

Mrs. Dworsky said, "I'm not that good at counting heads.

If you turn up one short, I'm not pawing through that muck to find the missing one."

"Diane can," said Steven.

"No rough stuff," Diane told him, "or you won't be invited back."

"Aren't you coming in?"

She knew from last year that the pond was muddy. She also knew that sometimes Mrs. Dworsky let her ducks in it to pull up weeds. "In a minute," she called to him. She turned to Tim. "Come on. I'll give you a tow."

"I don't want your toe," said crabby Tim.

"Not that kind," she explained. "I'll tow you on the tube, give you a ride."

Tim shook his head. He looked flushed. Did people exposed to rabies get red faces?

But he hadn't been exposed. No one had.

Steven made a fuss when she announced that she was taking them home. She told him Tim was feeling crummy, but that didn't arouse much sympathy.

"Looks fine to me," Steven declared. "He just likes attention."

The downhill walk home went a bit better until they turned in at the garden center. Tim went straight to Janet, who was potting a shrub for a customer. Her fingers on his cheek left traces of soil sticking to his damp skin.

"Juice," she said to Diane. "Inside, where he can stay cool. Downstairs. He can watch a video if he wants."

"Can I?" asked Steven.

Janet nodded, wiping the hair from her forehead and depositing smudges there, too.

"Can I choose?" Steven pressed.

"Diane!" Janet said meaningfully.

Diane reached for Tim, who yanked his arm from her grasp and glued himself to his mother. "Tim, you can let the puppy watch a video with you if you come right now," Diane told him.

He dragged himself out to the driveway and set off for the house.

When Steven raced past him, Diane called, "Steven, if you get there first, Tim still gets to choose."

Steven threw her a glowering look. "I know," he shouted. "I'm just going to get Tad."

Diane didn't bother to reply. Steven could talk his way out of almost anything. On a day like this it was easiest to let him get away with it.

21 The following afternoon Diane answered the phone when the vet called. He didn't want to leave a message. He said he was about to go out on some farm calls. He'd just stop by.

Since Tim was upstairs in bed, she asked Steven to stay inside while she delivered the message to his mom.

"Why can't I go?" he demanded. "I don't get to do anything when Tim's sick."

"He'll be better soon," she called back to him as she slammed out the door. Moss ran with her. Probably he was as bored as Steven and looking for some action.

"Did he say what time he'd be here?" Janet asked when Diane told her about the call.

"He's just leaving now. He's got farm visits. What does that mean?" Diane asked.

"It's like house calls," Rick told her. "Mostly it's easier for the vet to go to a sick cow than the other way around."

"Like with Dad's heifer," Janet added.

For a moment silence hung between them. Then Janet said to Rick, "Should I get Dad?"

Rick shook his head. "No need to jump the gun."

"But you know it's rabies," she said. "Otherwise Cliff would've just left word that the test was negative. Dad needs to hear what Cliff has to say as much as Steven does."

"One thing at a time."

"Even if Dad was exposed?"

"Janet," Rick said to her, "a rabid cat in the lamb pen doesn't add up to a rabid heifer that died."

"Died of unknown causes."

Rick drew a breath. "So call him then. Call Gordon."

Jace finished spraying the young evergreens and joined them. "I bet we get a storm soon," he said.

Rick didn't respond.

Jace said, "If there's lightning, someone better drive me home."

Rick nodded. Then he said, "The vet's stopping by. We may need you to stick around here for customers."

"I don't mind," Jace told him. "I just don't like lightning. I know someone that had a cousin that was struck."

"Really?" Diane exclaimed. "Killed?"

"No, but knocked out. Could've been killed. My sister's boyfriend knows another guy that—"

"You know what, Jace?" Rick told him irritably. "We don't need disaster stories today. Especially around the boys." He turned away.

Jace said to Diane, "If you ask me, those kids would be better off knowing what's out there."

Diane said, "They can't understand everything. Like right now when we say Tim's got a bug. Bugs are what he sees in the garden. He doesn't really know about bugs he can't see."

"People ought to pay more attention to stuff they can't see. You know what I think?" Jace told her. "I think that skunk had rabies. I was close to it, too. Remember?"

Diane nodded. "We can ask the vet when he's here."

"I'll do it," Jace said. "I got closer to it than you did."

"We'll both do it," she answered, trusting her own reporting more than his. "I saw it run over."

 "I can keep them quieter," Steven insisted, as Janet held the lambs for Dr. Canaday to examine. "They know me. I've been practicing for the junior sheep show at the fall fair."

His grandfather said, "That's good, Steven. But let Mom do it this time."

"What's the doc looking for?" asked Jace.

"Bites. Scratches."

"Any possible entrance site," the vet said as he bent over a lamb. "The virus is in the saliva of the rabid animal." He straightened. "You know, since raccoon rabies died down, we haven't seen any cases around till lately. Now there's a new fox strain coming down from Canada. A rabid coyote was shot in the valley a few weeks ago. Fortunately it wasn't buried until after the head was saved for testing. I expect we'll be seeing more cases around."

"Awhile back there was a skunk on the road," Jace told him. "It went after me."

Diane said, "It attacked a car. I saw it go for the front tire. It was run over." She didn't mention that Jace had provoked the skunk.

"Probably rabid," said Dr. Canaday.

"And right after that a cat was thrown out of a car. But I don't know if it was the same one. Could the cat I saw get rabies from the dead skunk?"

"It's possible," the vet told her. "If it ate part of the skunk's brain, that would do it."

Jace said, "But crows got that skunk."

Diane reminded him that he'd seen something drag part of it into the woods.

"Oh yeah. I forgot about that."

Dr. Canaday said, "Lyssa, the virus that produces rabies, can be transmitted to any other mammal during the symptomatic period of the disease. That means Gordon here should start on a course of treatment immediately."

Gordon said, "But that heifer never showed any aggression toward me. Actually, just the opposite. She did a lot of licking, like a dog."

Dr. Canaday shook his head. "I don't know what's worse, Gordon, people like you who keep so cool they run the risk of doing themselves in or people who shoot everything and anything just in case it carries a deadly virus. I'm sorry you didn't let me check out the heifer when her symptoms were more advanced. I guess you don't know that not all rabies cases are the furious kind. Licking is typical of some rabid behavior. Your heifer may have succumbed to something altogether different. But the risk of doing nothing is tremendous. Rabies has no cure. If you wait for the first symptoms, you're dead. And it's a terrible way to go."

"Dad!" said Janet.

"All right, all right," Gordon answered.

"As for the lambs," Dr. Canaday continued, "one leg has a scratch. Doesn't look fresh. But the cat might have jumped on their backs, dug its claws in, and bitten. Injuries like that are hard to detect. You could vaccinate them now and isolate them. But you're taking a chance."

Janet said, "I guessed we'd have to quarantine them for a while. They're Steven's project, you know."

"That's a pity," Dr. Canaday said to her and to Steven. "One of the frustrating aspects of the disease is its unpredictable incubation period. It can be as short as a couple of weeks, or it may last months before you know the animal is harboring the virus."

"So how would we dispose of them?" Janet asked him.

"Dispose of them?" Steven repeated. "What do you mean?"

"Steven, not now," Gordon told him. "We can talk after Dr. Canaday leaves."

"But what does she mean?" Steven's voice rose. "Send them away?"

Janet reached out to Steven, who yanked himself away. She turned to Jace. "I think Rick needs you at the center. And I'm going to need him here."

Steven planted himself in front of the vet. "Can't the lambs get the same treatment Grandpa's going to have?" He swung around to face his mother. "Ask how much it costs."

Dr. Canaday squatted down. "It's very complicated, son," he said gently. "Lots of things to consider. First there's safety. That comes way ahead of expense."

"So what will happen to them?" Steven demanded.

"What won't happen is the terrible suffering this disease causes every animal, man and beast. Even if these lambs get vaccine, one or both of them might still contract the disease. That would be far worse than a swift, painless end now."

Steven refused to look at him, at any of them. He said, "I knew that's what Mom meant. I knew it."

Tad came bounding into their midst, leaping first on Dr. Canaday, who was still crouched down at Steven's level.

"Hey, there!" the vet said, fondling the puppy. "I bet you're Steven's best friend."

Steven looked at Tad. "What about him?" he asked. "What are you going to do to him?"

Dr. Canaday stood up. "How old is he?"

Janet thought a moment. "Not yet three months. I was waiting for him to be old enough to be vaccinated."

Dr. Canaday nodded. "Any chance the cat could've come in contact with him?"

Janet frowned. "No. Well, maybe. We were away the day we found the cat. Tad was in his own pen. The grown dogs were with us."

For a moment no one spoke. Steven stood with clenched fists staring at the ground. Diane held her breath.

"You have to assume there's rabies around here. Deal with the lambs right off," Dr. Canaday said, walking toward his van. "Then make an appointment to get the puppy a shot."

Janet went along with him, and they stood for a moment, speaking quietly, before he got in and drove out to the road. When Janet returned, she said to Gordon, "How about a visitor for a day or so?"

"Fine," he said. "Steven will keep the women's minds off what I've got to do."

Janet said, "Call your doctor right now. From here."

"I'll do it when I get home," Gordon told her.

"Dad. Please."

"It's not fair!" Steven blurted. "Grandpa can go to the doctor, but you're going to shoot my lambs." He broke off. Then he said, "At least let me say good-bye to them."

"Didn't you hear a thing Dr. Canaday said?" Janet retorted. Then, softening her tone, she said, "Steven, I know this is hard on you. It's awful, and it's sad. Remember how we worried when the lambs were out all night and we heard the coyotes up the mountain? You know what might have happened to them, but it didn't. They were lucky. We were lucky. This time it's bad luck. But you know what? I bet Grandpa and Great-Gran Fennella can find two more lambs ready to be weaned that you can take on and get ready for the fall fair."

"I bet we can," Gordon said. "Get your things together, Steven. You and your great-grandmother can look over the flock."

"It's not the same," Steven declared in a choked voice. "I raised Aster and Nutmeg."

"You're right," Janet said. "There's nothing like caring for them from the start. But you'll have a project again." Turning to Diane, she asked her to pack some things for Steven. "There's laundry on the line you can take. I'll be right along. I just need a word with Rick."

Steven let his grandfather put an arm around his shoulders as they headed for the house. Diane detoured to the clothesline in back.

Tad followed her, then took off with a sock that had dropped to the ground. Diane refused to give chase. She folded T-shirts while she waited for the puppy to come close. When he pranced over to her, dangling and shaking the sock, she scooped him up in her arms and carried him inside along with the things Steven would need at the farm.

Steven joined Diane, who was upstairs looking for his backpack. The room was total chaos.

Tim jumped out of bed. "Who's here?" he asked.

"Your grandfather," Diane said.

"And the vet," Steven added.

"How come? I want to see them."

"You're supposed to stay in bed," Diane told him. "Steven, find your backpack."

"I feel better," Tim said. "I'm not sick anymore."

Steven pulled his backpack out from under Tim's bed. Diane turned it upside down and shook out pebbles and the remains of popcorn. Then she began to stuff the folded clothes in it.

"Where are we going?" Tim asked.

"Steven's going to the farm for a couple of days."

"Without me?" Tim demanded.

"They don't want me here," said Steven, returning from the bathroom with his toothbrush, "because they're going to shoot my lambs."

Tim sat back on his bed. "Why?" he asked. "What did the lambs do?"

"Nothing!" Steven retorted. "They didn't do anything at all."

"Steven," Diane said, "let your mom explain to Tim. Please."

"There's nothing to explain. I might as well take everything I own with me because I'm never coming back here." Steven stormed out of the room.

"He's going to live with Grandma and Grandpa and Great-Gran Fennella?" Tim asked.

"He's saying that because he's upset," Diane told Tim. "Really, he's going for a visit."

"It's murder," Steven bellowed from the stairs. "So watch out. You'd better not trust any grown-up, especially if they talk about disposing of something."

Tim ran out to the upstairs landing. "Steven," he shouted, "I don't know what you're talking about. Can I call you on the phone?"

Tad came scampering up the stairs. Blocked by Steven, the puppy slid back down, scrambling at each step to halt the descent.

"They say dispose when they mean shoot," Steven rasped. "Like Tad. He's in danger, because he isn't protected, so you'd better not let him out of your sight. Don't let them fool you either. They might tell you they're taking him to get a shot, you know, and you'll never see him again. That's what disposing is all about. Killing!"

"Steven," Janet said from downstairs, "come into the kitchen, please. Your dad and I want to talk with you before you go, and Grandpa needs to get back to the farm as soon as possible."

"Mom!" Tim yelled to her. "I'm all better. Can I come down, too?"

"I'm glad you're better," Janet called up to him. "But I want you to take it easy a bit longer. Maybe Diane will read to you."

Diane nodded to Tim. "You choose a book," she said.

Tim grabbed Tad and hauled him onto the bed. "Could you bring a string or a leash or something?" he asked her. "I want to keep Tad safe with me."

Diane went downstairs, glanced into the kitchen, and decided not to interrupt the intense discussion going on between Steven and his parents and grandfather. Back upstairs she pulled the belt from her bathrobe and brought it to Tim. "We can tie this to his collar for the time being. Just remember he needs to go outdoors a lot."

"How come Tad is in danger?" he asked.

"Because he's too young for the medicine that could protect him from rabies. Only he's nearly old enough. Soon he'll be safe, too."

"So rabies is real?"

Diane nodded. "Real," she said.

"And what Steven told me? That's real, too?"

Diane drew a breath. "Some of it is. About the lambs. But some of what he said is because he's upset."

Tim frowned. "When will the lambs be shot?" he asked.

"I don't know," she told him.

"Will it hurt?"

She said, "Your mother and father don't hurt animals. You know that."

"But they're going to shoot them."

"It has to be done." Diane tried to explain. She wished Janet and Rick would finish with Steven and come upstairs to Tim. "What do you want me to read?"

Tim hauled Tad onto the bed. The puppy burrowed in the tangled sheet.

"Don't let him chew," Diane warned.

Tim started to giggle. "Look," he said as the mound beneath the sheet bumped and lurched. "Tad thinks he's a ghost puppy."

"Don't forget what your dad said," Diane told him. "Ghosts aren't real."

"I know that," Tim told her brightly, "but Tad doesn't. Anyhow, it's just pretend."

Soon he and Tad were tussling under the covers. Diane left them to it. It was obvious that it wasn't going to be possible to keep Tim in bed much longer.

 Moss pushed through the kitchen door with Jace and went straight to Diane. He circled her twice and sat down on her feet.

"See," said Jace, "dogs can tell before a storm hits. I bet Tess is hiding out already."

A wind gust shook nearby branches. Something rattled across the porch.

"We're going to get it now," Jace declared ominously.

"It's just weather," Diane said, annoyed because he seemed to relish the prospect. It didn't compare with the family storm swirling all around them.

"Where did the cookies go?" Jace asked as he peered into a cupboard.

"I don't know," she snapped. "Before you start pigging out, would you take the puppy outside for a minute?"

"Why me? I just came in because I don't like thunder and lightning."

"You," she told him, "because you're here. I'm trying to fix a snack for Tim, who finally has an appetite again."

"All right," Jace said, "but the puppy better do his business right away. Where is he?"

"Upstairs. And don't make fun of Tim. He's worried about Tad."

Jace stomped up the stairs, and she turned her attention to the cheese sandwich she was grilling.

Jace came down carrying Tad. "Tim's convinced that

someone's about to take off with the puppy. So I promised to watch him every second," Jace told Diane. "Does that earn me a grilled cheese with ketchup?"

She nodded. Making two was just as easy as one. Besides, now she felt hungry for one herself.

Jace slammed back inside and set the puppy down. "Did everything," he said, flopping into a chair.

"Watch the oven," she told him as she carried a plate and a glass of apple juice upstairs. The puppy tore past her, at the mercy of momentum. "Don't tie him up now," she told Tim. "He needs to play for a while. And don't let him get your sandwich."

On her way down again, she could smell scorched bread. Jace was pushing away from the table as she dashed into the kitchen.

"I was getting it," he said.

He wasn't doing anything of the kind, but all she said was, "You'd better like well-done grilled cheese."

They ate in silence, listening to the first distant thunder. It sounded like a far-off sonic boom. Moss tried to crawl under Diane's chair.

"He thinks you can save him," Jace mumbled, his mouth full.

Diane reached down and pressed Moss close. That he came to her before anyone else filled her with happiness.

Janet and Rick made it inside just ahead of the first sharp thunderclap.

"Now's the time," Rick said softly.

Janet nodded. "Want me?"

"You be with Tim in case he hears."

But only Jace and Diane heard the shots. Three of them. Jace had to point out that three meant one must not have hit its mark on the first try. Diane suddenly regretted the grilled cheese sandwich. There was an awful taste in her mouth.

Janet came back downstairs. "Is it done?"

"Done," said Jace.

"Thanks to the storm, we didn't hear a thing," Janet said. "I'll go help bury them."

"I already dug the hole," Jace told Diane when she gave him a look. "I told them I'd do anything until thunder and lightning. Anyhow, there's no need to bury the lambs this minute."

"It beats leaving them there for Tim to see," Diane said.

Jace shrugged. "He knows they had to be shot. He knows why."

"He's scared," Diane replied. "It's confusing for a little kid. He has it in his head that Tad might be shot, too."

Rick opened the door and stood dripping on the thresh-hold. He told Jace to make a run for the truck.

It wasn't long before Diane heard the truck return. She looked outside. The storm, already subsiding, had left leaves strewn on the grass and a plastic bucket lying in the driveway. She saw Janet emerge from the barn and join Rick. Both were drenched. Yet they stood talking awhile in the falling rain.

Back in the house, they considered reopening the garden center, then decided they could do with an early night instead. Tim came downstairs to give Tad his supper, and Janet let him stand on the porch and watch while she took the puppy out for another run. Coming back to him, she said, "I'm glad you're better. Tad can stay with you tonight, so you won't be all alone."

It was still raining when swaths of clear sky began to

appear on the western horizon. All the while thunder rumbled across the mountain.

Moss, taking nothing for granted, clambered onto Diane's mattress and pressed close.

She slept profoundly, waking only once to find Moss at the door. She couldn't believe he needed to go out. "Lie down, Moss," she murmured. He would let her know if he really had to go.

But he sank back into sleep, and so did she.

 "Diane?"

What? Who? It was Janet, her voice low.

Diane's first thought as she opened her eyes in her windowless room was that she was late for their early-morning work session with Moss. "Coming," she replied.

"No," Janet said. "Not today. I just wondered if you have Tad."

Diane switched on the light. Moss was up, stretching, ready for the day.

"Isn't he with Tim?" she asked.

"I just opened the door a crack to call him out. I didn't want to wake Tim."

Diane looked at her watch. It was nearly eight. "I overslept," she said.

"We all did," Janet told her. "See you downstairs."

"What about the puppy?" Diane asked.

Janet said, "If there's a mess, it can be cleaned up. Let Tim sleep."

Diane put on her shorts and T-shirt and padded barefoot

down to the kitchen. She let Moss out and stood for a minute in the dazzling light. Everything looked fresh, the soaked land already almost dry under the sun-filled sky.

She turned back inside to join Janet and Rick. The kitchen smelled of coffee and toast.

"I think you'd better stick around here until you hear signs of life upstairs," Janet told her.

Diane, pouring orange juice for herself, said, "I'll probably hear from the puppy first."

Rick shoved a glass across the table, and Diane filled it. "Maybe not for a while, though," he said. "I found the puppy food out when I came down. Looks like Tim and Tad had themselves a midnight snack."

"Steven does that sometimes," Diane said.

"We know," the parents chorused.

"Well," Rick said, depositing his mug in the sink, "we'll leave it to you to wean Tim off daytime sleeping so that he gets through the night again. Have fun."

When they went out, Diane let Moss back inside. He flopped down near the door and watched her expectantly. "We're not working sheep this morning," she told him. "Everyone's wiped out after yesterday." Except Moss, she realized. Probably Tess, too. Once the thunderstorm had passed, the dogs were ready to go.

With Steven away and Tim asleep, the house seemed unnaturally quiet. Not even Tad was stirring. Diane's thoughts roamed from the puppy to the lambs to the cat. If it was the one she had seen in early May, where were its kittens? If they had survived this long, would their brief lives end in agony and death, too?

That idea was unbearable, so she picked up the telephone

and called home. No answer. She tried her aunt's house. After many rings Connie picked up.

"Why are you calling so early?" she drawled sleepily. "Something wrong?"

"It's not early," Diane said. "Where's Mom?"

"I don't know. At work?"

"Are you sure?" Mom didn't usually work the first shift.

"No. Wait a minute. I think she went with Mark. She was going to take some vacation days. I don't know, Diane. That might've been last week. Why don't you call tonight?"

"Any messages for me?" Diane asked.

"No. Yes. There was one from Zanna. Way back, though."

"Why didn't you call me? What did it say?"

Connie spoke through a yawn. "Nothing important. The usual."

The usual? There weren't that many e-mails for one to be considered usual.

After doing the few breakfast things, Diane leafed through pages and pages of brilliant pictures in one of Janet's seed catalogs. Still no sound from upstairs. Next she began to look at a black-and-white catalog that opened at the medicinal herb section. There seemed to be a cure for just about any ailment, or so the catalog claimed. Lemon balm uplifted the spirit. Feverfew prevented migraines. White yarrow was popular for colds and flu and also lowered blood pressure. Too bad there wasn't one to combat rabies.

Only what about this? An herb called mad-dog skullcap? Did Janet know that not only was this plant used as a nerve relaxant, but a tea made from its small blue flowers had once been believed effective against rabies? What would

Dr. Canaday say about that? He'd say there was no cure, absolutely none.

Diane read over the entire description again. The catalog writer had taken care to say that mad-dog skullcap was an old folk remedy. And Janet wanted to plant an entire garden of such plants? Diane tossed the catalog aside and glanced at her watch. It was nearly ten o'clock. Time to get the puppy out and maybe also to start Tim back on a daytime schedule.

No point keeping quiet anymore. But pounding barefoot up the stairs didn't seem to rouse the puppy or the boy. Opening the door a crack, she called Tad. Inside the room nothing stirred. She flung the door wide. The room was flooded with sunlight. It was empty.

She couldn't believe what she saw. "Tim," she shouted. "Tim." She didn't want to sound alarmed or cross, but she couldn't help herself. "Tim!"

Maybe he was hiding in the cellar. Moss followed her as she ran down to look, all the while calling Tim, calling Tad, and finding nothing. Still barefoot, she slammed out of the house and raced to the garden center.

 At first Janet and Rick couldn't believe that Tim wasn't just teasing, surely close by. Leaving Jace to serve customers, if any, they combed the house and barn and sheds, calling and calling. Diane tagged along after Janet, who asked the same questions over and over as if she believed that in time a useful answer would come.

But how could Diane help when she knew no more than they did?

Finally Janet called the farm and asked Dot to speak to Steven. "Don't alarm him," she said. "He's already upset." She turned to Rick. "Dad's at the doctor's. Mom wants to know if she should come. She can leave Steven with Fennella."

Rick shook his head.

"She's talking to Steven now. He might have an idea we haven't thought of."

But all Steven said was that Tim never went anywhere alone.

"Give Steven our love," Janet told her mother. "Yes, we will. We'll call neighbors first, though. Then the police."

For a moment she and Rick just stood looking at the telephone.

"This is unbelievable," Janet whispered. "I can't believe it's happening."

"You call," Rick said. "I'll go out on the road."

She said, "He knows about strangers. He knows about strange cars."

"I'll just drive where he might've been seen."

"If he left before sunup, no one would've seen him."

"We don't know when he left, Janet. Anyhow, he has the puppy. That should draw attention to him wherever he is. He can't get far."

As soon as Rick went out, Janet started to call the few households within walking distance. She kept her voice level, almost flat, as she explained to each person that her little boy had gone off somewhere with his puppy and had wandered out of earshot. If Diane hadn't seen Janet's taut mouth, the red blotches over her cheekbones, she would almost have believed that everything was under control.

She went upstairs to get her sneakers. At the same time she checked Tim's room again. If only he'd known how to write, she thought, as she pawed through his rumpled things. Since it was pointless to look for a note, what did she hope to discover? She had no idea.

Still, she had a vague sense that Tim might've left a clue. Her bathrobe belt, for instance, which she couldn't find. Had he taken it for a leash even though he would have been able to grab one downstairs? Also, where was his backpack? If he were planning to come home soon, he wouldn't bother with it. She crawled halfway under the bed and dragged out one toy after another before concluding that he must have it with him. That was when she thought of the puppy food he'd neglected to put away. What else had he stowed in his backpack before taking off? Well, the heavier the better. Lugging stuff would slow him down.

In less than an hour the driveway was clogged with pickups and cars. Neighbors, near and distant, were joining the search. First off, the police wanted all hazards checked, mostly backyard swimming pools and farm ponds.

More cars drove up. People came and went. Word had gotten out about the rabies. Diane overheard scraps of wildly inaccurate information. Some people feared rabid animals lurking in the woods. That was an area that should be reserved for men with guns. Mrs. Dworsky suggested that the odds were against anyone's coming face-to-face with another rabid animal. It was like the odds against lightning's striking twice in the same place. Jace spoke up at once. His grandfather heard of someone getting struck twice, burned the first time, killed the second.

Most people were sent to search areas they were familiar with, but some objected. The kid had to be close by. Unless he'd been picked up.

"Picked up?" Diane repeated.

"Kidnapped," Jace said. "Stolen."

Heat rushed into her face. "No!"

"I didn't say I thought he was," he told her.

"Anyone look in the Pederson house?" asked Mrs. Dworsky.

"He'd never go there," Jace told her. "He knows about the Pederson ghost."

"Still," she insisted, "not every kid believes that drivel. Ought to be checked."

A police sergeant said, "You're talking about the property downhill that's just been sold?"

Mrs. Dworsky nodded. "Our neighborhood haunted house, about to be demolished." She fixed Jace with a look. "Someone who knows it should have a look."

"Someone with a car," Jace retorted.

The police sergeant surveyed the group of volunteers. "Who'll go?" he asked.

"I'll drive Jace over," Mrs. Dworsky said. "There's my car."

"Let's have one more person. Tony?"

"Tony the Batman!" Mrs. Dworsky exclaimed as a man Diane didn't know stepped forward, clapped a huge hand on Jace's skinny back, and said, "Let's go!"

Caught by surprise, Diane echoed, "Batman?"

"Last time around," Mrs. Dworsky explained, "Tony decided to stamp out rabies single-handed by killing all the bats. He must've bagged a thousand of them."

"Didn't work," someone else remarked. "The epidemic ran its course."

"No shotguns, no rifles," the sergeant responded. "Not with so many people searching."

Jace made one feeble attempt to duck out. "You know that house is haunted," he said.

Tony wasted no time. Propelling Jace toward Mrs. Dworsky's car, he said, "Rabies scares me a lot worse. It ought to scare you, too."

Diane stepped aside as another search party was formed. Moss came to her, looking up the way he did when he was asking for work. "Not now," she told him quietly. Then a thought struck her: Moss! She wasn't thinking about some dorky Disney movie about a dog rescuing its owner. She was recalling how Moss had caught on about finding the puppy. If before, why not now? And if he could follow Tad's trail, wouldn't that lead to Tim?

27

Since no one she knew was in sight, she ran to the house and scribbled a note: "Moss with me." Now what? she wondered. If she was going to make Moss understand, they ought to be away from all distractions. But should she wait for the volunteers to clear out? The longer she postponed sending Moss on the search, the less chance he had of picking up a scent.

She thought of Tim's trying to catch up with her the day she followed Moss into the woods. Since the only thing he'd been afraid of was being left behind, she doubted that the woods would have deterred him. And if he hadn't gone this way, wouldn't Moss let her know?

Once again with Moss at her side, she skirted the new garden area and climbed over the stone wall. The woods buzzed with mosquitoes. She tried to imagine Tim fighting them off and then tried to erase what she imagined. Anyway, if he had taken off in this direction, it was probably before the sun had begun to penetrate the leaf cover, so it might not have been so bad.

"Look!" she told Moss. "Look, look back!"

He darted away, then stopped a few yards ahead of her and turned. He was waiting for further direction, and she didn't know what to say. Maybe he needed to be connected to something of Tim's. Maybe Tim had entered the woods below the new garden area, so there was no scent here for Moss to pick up. Or maybe he had gone another way entirely.

Moss was poised to run. What else had she told him last time when he had gone after the puppy? It came to her in a flash. Moss had understood she was seeking Tad because she had called him. That's what she had to do now.

First she used the puppy call that had brought the whole litter running for their food. Then she used Tad's name. Moss looked ahead, looked at her, looked ahead. This time when she told him to find Tad, to look and look, he trotted around in a semicircle until he was moving toward the house.

Her heart sank. "Moss, no," she said. She went to him, grabbed his collar, and shoved him so that he faced into the woods again. Still holding him, she repeated her Tad and puppy calls. When she released him, he looked all about, then moved off, but without much confidence. At least it was a start. At least she could keep up with him. "Good boy, Moss," she told him. "Look, look. Puppy Tad. Good boy."

The farther they went, the harder it was to follow him. He could get through and under tight places that blocked her. "Moss," she called as he vanished and reappeared on a zigzag course. She didn't dare call him back or even ask him to stay long enough to let her catch up.

Her soaked sneakers were black with mud; her legs were scratched bloody. She didn't even feel the mosquitoes glued to them. All that mattered was not losing sight of the black-and-white dog, so hard to see in the dark undergrowth.

Every time shafts of sunlight sliced through that darkness, she hoped that it signaled a change. Maybe the woods were thinning. Maybe Moss was approaching open land. But time and again the light simply blinded her, sometimes sending her slamming into a stone or a tree trunk or a tangle of briars. Each time she was stopped, she cried out, "Moss!" Then she picked herself up and staggered on.

By the time she broke through the trees into an overgrown meadow dotted with red cedars and thistle and mullein, tears were blurring her eyes, and she nearly missed catching sight of Moss. He was downhill from her and trotting purposefully toward a weathered gray house that looked as if it were about to sink into the ground. The Pederson house? It couldn't be any other.

"Moss. Stay there," she called to him. She needed to catch her breath.

He stopped, looked back at her, and waited.

She knew that Jace and Mrs. Dworsky and the big man called Tony must have been there already. If Tim had been inside, he would have been found. Was he all right?

She could make her way to the road to find out, but it seemed only fair and right to let Moss finish what he had begun.

This time she didn't have to run. Moss went straight to a side window, once boarded up and now broken with only a single remaining slat nailed across the top. A rusted bin beneath it might have served as a step. Could Tim have climbed inside? Moss thought so. On his hind legs, he peered through.

"Stay," she told him once more.

His ears pricked as something creaked inside. Even she could hear it over the constant hum that droned from within. One look at the interior plastered with bird droppings and rotted timbers suggested that the sound could be coming from almost anything. As far as she could tell, a good part of the floor had fallen away. A woodstove, suspended over the broken floor, was barely attached to a pipe that had once led to the chimney.

Diane didn't relish the idea of entering the place, but she had to be sure she wasn't missing anything. She went around to the front, and the first thing she saw was the irrigation pipe that Rick had used to batten the door closed. When she looked inside through a front window, she could see the same room and another one on the other side of the chimney. This one had a sink against the back wall and a tilted table propped on two legs. A door stood open at the farther end. Craning, she was able to see a landing and a few upright crosspieces, nothing more. She guessed it was a cellar door, although no steps were visible.

So that was that. Tim had braved this creepy place, and poor Jace, who dreaded coming here, probably had had to help fetch him out.

Making her way through the weeds, she called to Moss. It would be a lot easier going back to the road once she got to the part of the driveway that had been cleared for vehicles. Moss came to her, then turned back. "That'll do," she told him. "You were right on target. But it's all over. Tim and Tad aren't there anymore."

Moss stood his ground. He started back to the house. "Moss, come!" she ordered.

Ignoring the command, he turned away from her. She thought, all right, maybe he deserved to see for himself that Tim and Tad were no longer there. She went with him. It wouldn't take long.

She put her foot right through the bin that Tim must have used to climb inside. It didn't matter. She could shimmy over the crumbling sill. Moss cleared it, but the flooring he landed on buckled and snapped. "Stay," Diane whispered. Why whisper? They weren't hiding from anyone. In response to something she couldn't see or hear, Moss thumped his tail against the wall, sending forth a spray of dust and paint flakes. Then came the unmistakable whimper of a puppy.

"Tad?" she shouted. Why had the rescuers left the puppy behind when they brought Tim out? The house reeked of rot and worse. The floor felt as flimsy as the bin she had stepped through. Figuring it was strongest along the outside wall, she went that way. "Tad," she called again.

Another stifled whine led her toward the jagged hole in the center of the floor. At the sound of wood splintering, she dropped down and crawled on her hands and knees. When she finally got close enough to see some of what lay below, she stopped to cover her mouth and nose. The stench rising from the cellar was powerful enough to squeeze the breath out of her.

She had to orient herself, get used to the idea that she

was kneeling over some kind of grave. Bones lay strewn, some of them still partly connected. She saw a rib cage and a spine with head attached, the head with shreds of hair or fur, she couldn't tell which. In the midst of this collection of dead things, Tad scrambled onto a skull and gazed up at her. He was trailing her bathrobe belt.

She guessed he had fallen through. She said, "Didn't Tim tell them you were here?"

Tad yipped excitedly.

How could Tim have left the puppy behind? She couldn't make sense of it. Had Tim been hurt and unable to speak? Or had he still been trying to conceal Tad from those he thought might hurt him? Shoot him?

Backing up, hugging the wall again, she tried to walk around to the stove. Tad whined. She said, "All right. Good boy. I'm looking for a way down." Behind the stove a floorboard angled up, exposing rusted nails loose in their holes. But that wasn't all that it exposed. She found that she could see straight down. And there was a familiar sneaker. More than that, Tim's leg. She shrieked. The leg jerked. "Tim!" she cried. "Tim, you're there! Are you all right?"

Finally he answered. "Sort of. Not really. My arm hurts a lot. When I fell, everything came down all at once. But I fooled the people that came. I stopped crying. I kept Tad quiet. They went away."

"Oh, Tim, you've scared us to death. You have to come home now."

"I can't," he told her.

"But nothing's going to happen to Tad. Really."

"Steven said everyone would say that. Even Jace acted like Tad was in danger."

"It's a mixup," Diane told him. "I'll explain as soon as you come out."

"I can't," he said again. Then he added, "My leg's stuck underneath part of the stairs. It doesn't hurt, though. I just can't push off all the stuff."

Diane could feel panic surge through her. She knew she mustn't frighten him. Forcing herself to sound offhand, she asked him how he had got down there.

"Stairs," he told her. "They broke, though. They fell apart. I held Tad partway."

"Just a minute," she said. "I'm going to look." But when she cautiously made her way to the kitchen, the stairwell she had glimpsed from the front window yawned just as blackly as before.

Testing the landing, she leaned over, then drew back. The stairs were a jagged mess. If she jumped from there and landed on that heap of splintered debris, she could end up worse off than Tim.

All right, she thought. Everything would be all right. She could go for help. She would explain the situation, and rescuers would come with a ladder and ropes. "Tim," she called down to him, "I have to tell people you're here."

"No!" he cried.

"Yes. I promise it'll be fine. It won't take long."

"Don't go," he pleaded. "Don't leave me."

"I'll come back." She could hear him sobbing. She realized that he was terrified. He didn't want to be found, but he didn't want to be left either.

"Listen, Tim," she called to him, "I'll leave Moss with you. He'll keep you and Tad company till I get back. He won't let anything bad happen. You know you can count on him to protect you both. Tim, did you hear me? I'm going now. I'm going to tell Moss to stay."

Diane was at the front door, but she couldn't push it open. She had to creep back to the window. "Moss, stay," she said, and slithered out. Thrusting her way to the rutted driveway, she started to shout long before she reached the road. A man she didn't know ran toward her. She gasped out her news and the need for ropes and a ladder. The man raced uphill and was almost out of sight when she stopped for breath beside Mrs. Dworsky's car.

The man yelled at someone off to the side, and Tony stepped onto the road. He ran down the hill and would have passed her if she hadn't stopped him. "You need ropes and maybe a ladder," she told him. "That man's going for them."

"I've seen the place. I can't believe we missed the kid. If there's a way to get to him, I'll find it." He pushed past her.

She called after him, "Wait! Tim's really upset. He doesn't know you."

Tony shouted something and kept going.

Jace loped toward her. "Is Tony going back to the Pederson house?"

Diane told him about Tim and the puppy.

"No way. We looked inside. Are you sure?"

Diane nodded. "I told Tony that someone's gone for a ladder and ropes. I asked him to wait. Can you stop him? I should get there first."

"That guy's a nutcase," Jace told her. "Thinks he's some kind of big-time hero. He'd kill to be the one that saves the lost kid."

"Jace, please. Tim's so scared already, and I promised I'd be back." Her legs were trembling. "Hurry," she implored as Jace went tearing after the big man. She made herself return to the driveway and began to follow him.

She was fighting her way through the brambles and brush when she heard shrieks coming from the house. She plunged on, ripping her clothes, her skin, even her hair. Now she could see Jace, who was just inside the door, which hung open, lopsided.

"You do like I said!" Tony bawled at Jace above the continuous clamor from within. She saw Jace lunge forward. He was shoved so hard he fell backward onto the ground.

Jace rolled over and sat up. "Diane!" he gasped. "Moss went at him. He's after Moss. He wants someone with a gun. Diane!"

She pounded up to him. "Are you all right?" she asked.

He gestured at the house, where separate voices were beginning to emerge through the din: Tim shrieking, "Get him, get away, get him," Tad's shrill yipping, Tony hurling threats, and savage, deep-throated growls.

Diane burst inside. Tony, his back to the open door, swung the irrigation pipe at Moss, who faced him, snarling.

"Get back," Tony yelled at her. "Out of here."

"Get him!" Tim screamed.

Never had Diane seen Moss like this, his eyes burning, his lips drawn back so far that he looked all teeth and slathering rage.

"Stop!" Diane yelled at the man. "Moss," she cried. "That'll do, Moss."

The instant Moss turned aside and dropped his guard, Tony slammed the pipe against him. The impact lifted Moss off his precarious perch. He yelped once before dropping to the cellar below.

Sickened, Diane stood frozen, unable to utter a sound.

"Diane!" Tim called to her. "Help. Help Moss."

"Don't go near that dog," Tony called down to him. "He's dangerous. Understand? He attacked me." He turned to Jace, who had come inside. "What's the matter with you? I told you I had a mad dog in here. Well," he added, "if he's still alive, I guess he's not going anywhere."

Diane couldn't look at the man. She couldn't speak to him. Without a word, she crawled toward her earlier observation spot in front of the stove.

Tony tried to stop her. He pointed out that if she fell through the floor near the dog, she could be bitten. "That's like a death sentence," he told her.

Peering down, she finally located Moss inert on the heap of bones. Tad skirted his body, pawing and nuzzling at him.

Behind and above her other voices approached. "Ropes coming," she said to Tim, who asked hoarsely if Moss was dead.

She stared at the dog. It was so dark down there. Moss was so still. Had his head moved because Tad had nudged him? She couldn't tell.

29

Despite Tony's assertion that he should be the first to go down to the cellar, Diane and Jace prevailed. Since she was the lightest person and the one Tim trusted the most, she was allowed to go first.

As she was lowered into the stairwell, she could hear Tony defending himself, still maintaining that all he had done was try to keep a mad dog from the trapped child.

"How was I to know?" he blustered. "There's a little kid all alone down there, and this crazy dog after me. The boy himself was crying for help. Isn't that right?" he insisted, calling on Jace to back him up. "You heard him yell at me to get him." Someone else spoke in lower tones. "Well, what if the dog was rabid and I didn't take things in hand like I did?" Tony demanded. "Everyone would blame me."

The man holding the rope reminded Diane to watch out for nails. Someone else said that Rick was on his way. So was an ambulance. Other people were looking for Janet, who was still out searching.

Diane kept reaching for supports that collapsed. When she started to haul herself onto a solid beam, Tim cried out, and she realized that his leg was pinned under the other end of it. She slid off and crept around it. She had to shove his backpack aside to reach him, careful not to touch the arm that hurt. He was shivering, so she cradled his head, brushing away the flies that clung to him. Tad came wriggling over to her, ecstatic and silly, as if it were perfectly natural to meet an old friend in a wildlife graveyard under a house.

She explained to the people above about Tim's injured arm and his stuck leg, and they told her not to try to shift the beam. The fire department was bringing a stretcher. Tim, stuttering because of chattering teeth, begged her to see about Moss. But she stayed with him until she heard the firefighters being lowered down with the stretcher and first aid.

The stench made her stomach heave. Or maybe it was feeling all the carcasses she had to drag herself over that brought her to the brink of nausea. When she reached Moss, she choked back a cry of horror. One side of his head was a mass of blood and bone. Flies crawled over it, too groggy to take to their wings. In spite of their hideous buzzing, his rapid breaths came through to her. They sounded like the last desperate gasps of a tiny animal.

Right after Tim on the stretcher had been hoisted up, she heard Rick speaking to him. Tim, his voice piercingly high, pleaded for Tad. "No," he wailed, "with me." She guessed the puppy was handed over to him because he didn't say another word.

Now Rick was talking to someone else. But there were too many voices at once, and she couldn't make out what he said.

In a little while she heard the ambulance siren. Someone called down and asked if she could get back to the stairwell on her own. They had a ladder secured there now for climbing out. She answered that she needed to stay with the dog until the vet came. He had been sent for, hadn't he?

There was some discussion above. To her astonishment, Jace spoke up, offering to hang out there so Diane wouldn't be alone while she waited.

"You all right?" he asked her after the others had gone. "It's not freaking you out being with all those stinking dead things?"

"I'm all right," she said, no longer fighting off the flies that stuck to her scratched legs and arms and head. "How about you?" she managed to ask him.

"Well," he drawled, "I guess I'm better off than you. Even Rick admitted it's no place to be. Did you hear him telling the others about it?"

She shook her head.

"Diane? Did you hear what Rick said?"

"No," she told him.

"Seems like he's known some winters when this door's blown open and deer come for shelter and fall through the floor and starve. He was saying he's always been afraid of a person getting trapped like them. Can you believe that? Rick afraid, though he still doesn't think it's haunted, even after his own kid is the one that lands in trouble here. Diane? Did you hear me?"

She said she did. Only she didn't want to talk. She just wanted to be next to Moss in case he felt her quiet presence and sensed that she wouldn't leave him.

Time stalled, the present measured by Moss's quick, shallow gasps. If only she could draw one deep, full breath for him.

Floorboards above her creaked. The vet? But it was only Jace moving about. He couldn't quit fidgeting. He cleared his throat, started to whistle, then stopped.

"You okay?" he asked.

"Yes."

"Maybe I should wait out by the road to show the vet where to come."

Diane nodded.

"Diane, what do you think? Would you be all right?"

"Yes."

But Jace hesitated. "I told them I'd stay with you," he said. "Only what if Dr. Canaday doesn't know—"

"Oh, go, Jace. Please."

She listened to him leave. She listened to Moss struggle for air. She listened to a world of flies, all intent on feeding. Then she heard footsteps and voices. At last.

When Dr. Canaday and his reluctant assistant finally descended with emergency equipment, she let her tears go. They streamed down her face and onto her hands and legs.

Dr. Canaday tapped and listened and pulled up Moss's eyelids and tapped some more. Finally he spoke: "The humane thing to do is put him down."

Diane shook her head, the tears unchecked.

"He's not Janet's, is he?" Dr. Canaday said. "I seem to recall something like that." He filled a syringe and injected a clear liquid into a vein in Moss's foreleg. "He's yours?" he asked Diane. At her answering nod, he said, "It doesn't look good. We won't know exactly what's fractured till we get him X-rayed, but he's certainly broken some ribs. I'm afraid we're dealing with a punctured lung. If we could get him to a major animal clinic, maybe—"

Diane gazed at him. Why didn't he tell her what he could do, not what he couldn't?

He looked from the dog to Diane. "I can't make any promises. Most bones can mend, but we'll have to see the extent of the internal injuries. And he may not survive being moved."

She nodded again. She said, "He found Tim. He did."

"Right," said Dr. Canaday. "We'll give it our best shot."

Carrying and lifting Moss out of the cellar hole, Dr. Canaday and his assistant spoke in medical terms she couldn't understand. She wished they would tell her what pulmonary contusions meant and what the dexamethasone was supposed to do for Moss. Did they see that blood was dripping from his nose? Why didn't they clean off the side of his head where a bone protruded? But she didn't say a word because they were treating him even as they settled him in the van, and she was afraid to interfere in any way.

Dr. Canaday wasn't prepared to take her along with the dog, but she climbed into his van, anyway. Then at the animal clinic she was left in the small reception room to wait.

To her surprise Jace showed up on his bike with Cokes and potato chips. She didn't think she could stand any food, but when he opened the bag, she dug in, devouring its contents so quickly that he barely got a mouthful for himself. "Thanks," she mumbled, spraying crumbs as she spoke. "Did you bring anything else?"

Jace shook his head. "I told Janet where you and Moss were. Tim's okay. His arm's broken, is all. You're supposed to call when you're ready to go home."

"Thanks," she said again. Then she added, "Considering how you feel about the Pederson house, it's cool how you hung out there."

"Oh," he said without meeting her eyes. "Maybe I shouldn't've left you. I mean, I figured the ghost wouldn't stay around with all that commotion. Still, it's no place . . ." His voice fell away. "Anyway, I'd better get home." Already he was backing toward the door. "My folks worry when I'm out on my bike after dark," he said, as if sharing a joke with her.

A long time later Dr. Canaday walked into the reception area and sat down slowly. He said, "That dog was severely injured some time ago. I'm surprised he's still been able to work."

Diane nodded. "I know. He was hit by a car or torn up by coyotes. It was my fault. I'm the one that sent him for sheep that coyotes were after."

"He was lucky to survive," Dr. Canaday said. "I'd be surprised if his heart isn't compromised. We'll just have to wait and see whether his luck holds."

Again he warned her not to raise her hopes too high. He

wouldn't let her near Moss, who needed to be kept completely quiet. Even if the dog lived, he wouldn't be running after anything—not livestock, predators, or even grasshoppers—anytime soon.

 Fennella, who came for Diane, exchanged a word or two with Dr. Canaday about the heifer, about Gordon.

"Well, Cliff, this'll teach me to put off fence repair," she said dryly. "If the heifers hadn't strayed, we wouldn't be in this fix."

"You mean Gordon would've been spared," Dr. Canaday commented. "It wouldn't have changed what happened since the dead cat showed up in the Pragers' lamb pen."

Diane said, "I should've told somebody about the skunk. About the cat. At least we might've saved its kittens."

Dr. Canaday shook his head. "There's no telling how one thing may lead to another. Think what you might've brought into the Prager family if you'd saved the cat. Once it was incubating rabies, it was a time bomb."

"What about the kittens?" she asked.

Dr. Canaday shrugged. "I'd hope for their sake they didn't last very long." Turning to Fennella, he changed the subject. "How's Steven doing?"

"Coming around. Except he feels responsible for Tim overreacting."

"Sounds like quite a few people overreacted." Dr. Canaday nodded toward Diane. "This one dug in her heels, wouldn't let me put down the dog. So we've done what we could. Understand, though, we're not home free. A displaced fractured rib bone did a lot of damage. We didn't repair the pelvic fracture because they usually heal on their own in four to six weeks. But this one included the hip joint, and that's bound to create serious problems. Even without further surgery, saving this dog will cost a pretty penny."

"You need to be paid now?" Fennella asked.

He shook his head. "Just so long as everyone understands that it's not over. Not by a long shot."

On the way out to Fennella's truck, Diane said, "That's the sort of thing that Tim might hear wrong. He keeps trying to figure out what's real and what's imaginary. 'Long shot.' When he's already confused, he makes the wrong connection."

"Well, he needs help taking all this in. If you ask me," Fennella continued, "Rick and Janet ought to cut back their garden center hours and spend more time with the boys."

Diane said, "That's supposed to be my job."

Fennella glanced her way. "Exactly."

Fennella criticizing Janet and Rick? Diane rose to their defense. "I think they're awesome parents."

Fennella grunted. "Probably are. Still, the way I see it, most good parents are like most good farmers: They seldom measure up to their own best intentions." She paused for a moment, then added in steely tones, "Nor are they as wanting as their critics make them out to be."

Diane was too drained to figure out exactly what Fennella was saying. She stared ahead. Houses and barns sped by, barely glimpsed in the headlights' beam before darkness engulfed them. She was left with an eerie impression that they hovered above the road's surface. She thought of Jace pedaling through the night, hurrying home because his parents worried, probably about traffic. "He still believes there's a ghost," she murmured. "Jace."

"Lots of people believe in ghosts," Fennella replied.

"Do you?" Diane asked her.

Fennella said, "Depends. I don't believe in Halloween spooks, but I do believe that the living are sometimes haunted. And not always by the dead."

"What do you mean?" Diane exclaimed.

"Well, take Zanna. She's surely haunted Moss, especially when she first moved away. I think she's been haunting you, too."

"Oh." Diane didn't know what to make of that notion. But it reminded her that she needed to square something away. "I told Dr. Canaday that Moss was mine."

"I see," Fennella said. "That gave you the authority to insist on trying to save him?"

"I had to," Diane told her. "Moss was there because I made him stay with Tim."

"And then, as I understand it, you stayed with Moss," Fennella added. "I expect that makes you his, at least for the time being."

Through the blur of exhaustion Diane let that statement sink in. It wasn't about ownership. That much got through to her. Maybe it was about belonging and the obligation attached to it. "So I'll have to pay the vet bill?" Diane said.

"Something will be worked out," Fennella told her. "There's a fair number of people who agree with your stand. Beginning," she added, "with my dear Rob, who would surely haunt me and make my life miserable if I let Moss down."

Diane kept forgetting that Moss had belonged to Fennella's husband before Zanna became his next loving owner. After Zanna there had been a mystery caretaker, who had kept Moss and then had let him go. Since then Moss, left in Janet's capable hands, watched every car, every person who came to the garden center. Waiting to be claimed? Rob was dead now, Zanna far away, and the mystery person vanished.

But Diane was here. Was that what Fennella was saying?

When Diane walked into the Pragers' house, for one uneasy moment she felt like a stranger. Then Tess stretched and rose to greet her. Rick at the door said that Janet had already talked with Cliff Canaday and was upstairs running a bath for Diane.

Fennella declined the supper kept warm on the stove. It was past her bedtime, she said. Diane, drawn into Fennella's bony embrace, was too tense and stiff to respond. "Take care of this girl," Fennella told Rick. "Bloody but unbowed she may be, but she could still do with a strong dose of comfort."

Before she had her bath, Diane had to check on Tim, curled up with Tad. They looked like two puppies drawing comfort from each other. Comfort. Fennella's word.

Janet warned Diane that with all her scratches and scrapes the bath water might sting. But Diane felt only the enveloping heat and a tingling that reminded her that she was still able to feel. She seemed to have cast off more than the grime and sweat of this harrowing day. What was it Fennella had said about her belonging to Moss? As though a debt had been paid.

Twice Janet stopped at the bathroom door to ask Diane if she was all right. "Don't fall asleep in there," she said.

When Diane finally came downstairs, holding her bathrobe closed because it was missing its belt, she was presented with an array of casseroles, offerings from neighbors. Diane sampled small helpings of tuna and noodles and chicken and rice, but she couldn't eat much.

Janet said, "Never mind. It'll be here tomorrow."

"And the day after," said Rick. "And so on."

"Not with Steven home again," Janet said.

"And Jace having two lunches," added Diane.

All three of them sounding perfectly normal. There was comfort aplenty in that.

31

On a hazy morning at the end of August, Mrs. Dworsky drove up to the Prager house and unloaded a crate from the back of her pickup. "Where do you want them?" she asked Janet, who was already digging in the new garden.

"See how they like the wading pool," Janet called back. Rising, she brushed soil from her knees, then joined Diane, who was already helping to carry the crate across the lawn.

Steven and Tim ran out onto the porch, the screen door banging behind them.

Mrs. Dworsky told them to stand back. Then she opened the end and tipped the crate. Five babbling long-necked ducks waddled upright onto the grass. In single file they marched flat-footed like mechanical toys toward the wading pool.

"You'll have to keep changing the water," Mrs. Dworsky told the boys.

Steven said, "If they stay here, maybe we can get a bigger pool."

"One thing at a time," Janet said. "We don't even know whether Moss can handle them. They're temporary, just to ease him back to work. Diane, want to bring him out?"

During the six weeks since his return home, the living room had become Moss's place, his and Diane's. Even before he was allowed to stay out of his crate, she had moved downstairs to be with him at night.

Her mother had come to see her, to make sure that everything at the Pragers' really was all right. Since there had been only one other verified case of rabies in the area, a fox caught in a chicken coop, Diane's mother had set aside anxiety to look askance at Diane's sleeping arrangement.

It struck Diane as strange that back in June she had worried about Mom's reaction to the windowless room upstairs. Even though Diane had loved her small, private space, it didn't seem important anymore. All that mattered was staying with Moss and taking care of him.

Her mother had made an effort to understand. "Are you happy?" she had asked. "You want to stay on?"

Happy? Diane didn't know how to describe how she felt. But she responded fervently to the second question. She needed to be here. That was how she put it to her mother, who went home a little baffled but somewhat reassured.

Since her mom's visit, Diane had become more aware of time passing, of the new school year just ahead. She wished she could prepare Moss for her absence, but there was no way to show him what was to come. All she could do was urge him on in his struggle for strength and mobility. Like now, when he was to be given a chance to try a little duck herding.

When she called Moss into the kitchen, he hauled himself to his feet, took a moment to establish his balance, then hobbled after her. She took him out the back door with its single step down to the ground and then around the house.

Mrs. Dworsky said, almost too brightly, "He's looking much better."

"Some better," Janet replied, "for a dog that'll be permanently lame." She was frowning. "He may not be ready for even a small duck-herding demonstration."

"Let him try," pleaded Steven. "We need to practice for the fair."

Still frowning, Janet walked to the far side of the wading pool, shooed the ducks away from it, and told Moss to fetch them.

As soon as he turned away to circle behind them, they veered out of his path. Slowly he moved to block them. Too slowly. The ducks gained speed. Moss did not. Janet whistled softly, telling him to flank to the right. He obeyed, but by the time he got himself into a better position, the quacking ducks were scattering noisily. Ordering him to stay, Janet called off the experiment.

"It's too soon," she said. "We can always try later. But we need to rethink the demonstration. And, Steven, we have to face facts. We can't put in endless time and effort on a dog whose trialing days are over."

Diane was aghast. Moss was poised to continue, to finish the job. Even if he couldn't understand Janet's words, he must sense their meaning.

Mrs. Dworsky took in Steven's downcast expression. "Still," she said, "it wasn't that bad. I mean, for a first attempt. Was it?"

Janet shook her head. "Moss won't be good enough for the fair."

"He's good enough for me," Diane blurted.

"I'm supposed to do the demo," Steven told her. He turned to his mother. "It's not fair if Diane takes over. Unless," he added, "I can use Tess."

Diane said, "I'm not taking him to any fair."

Janet said, "Okay, Steven. Maybe you're ready to handle Tess now."

The ducks said whatever ducks say when a wild puppy hurtles toward them.

And Tim said, "Look at Tad. He's already better than Moss."

Tad, transformed mid-leap from chasing terror to novice herder, had dropped to a crouch. Creeping forward, he swung wide and scrambled as fast as his young legs could carry him until he held the protesting ducks in a tight group.

Janet scooped him up. She said, "Very promising, but I think we'll get Tess to put the ducks back in their crate." Tad squirmed, trying to free himself. She said to him, "Next year, maybe, you little monster. Grow a bit, mellow out, and Steven will be begging to run you at the fall fair."

"What about this year?" Steven pressed. "Will you help me get Tess ready? Since I can't use Moss?"

Moss, who hadn't moved since Janet called a halt to the experiment, was still eyeing the ducks. Diane knew he would go on eyeing them, even after Tess was called to replace him. "I'll crate the ducks," she declared. Could she? Would Moss be able to help?

While the others stood waiting for her to get the job done, she asked Moss to bring the ducks. His awkward, side-thrusting gait seemed to unnerve the ducks even more than the explosive puppy had. They flapped into one another in their haste to escape him.

"Stay," she told him. She ran around to the crate, dragged

it to the wading pool, and lifted it into the water. "Now, easy," she said to the dog. He was on the verge of losing them to the opposite flank when she caught on. He couldn't bend and turn fast enough. She had to become another sheepdog, working across from him. Together they crowded the ducks against the edge of the pool until, one by one, they tumbled over the side and splashed toward the open crate.

"Good boy," she said to him as she shoved the last two inside and closed them in. "That'll do, Moss."

"That's not how to pen," Steven told her. "You're not supposed to do that much."

She led Moss back to the house. She didn't need to be informed that she hadn't penned properly. "It worked," she murmured as she let him into the kitchen. "You worked. It's what we can do, the two of us."

Moss flopped down, spent. When she brought the water bowl to him, he made no effort to get up but lapped awkwardly before stretching out on his side. She sat there awhile, stroking him, telling him how good he was to have finished what he had begun. Forget the ribbons and trophies he would never again compete for. There would always be some task for him to perform.

Would that be enough? Was she enough? Sitting cross-legged beside him, she had to remind herself that if he was maimed because of her, he was alive because of her as well.

"Moss," she whispered to the dog lying on the kitchen floor. His tail thumped. Shoving his muzzle at her knee, he let out a long sigh. Then he lifted one forepaw and placed it lightly on her arm.

Was it up to him then? Had she missed the point, worrying over dead Rob and absent Zanna and the mystery caretaker? Of course they would always haunt Moss. Maybe that was what Fennella had been getting at the night he nearly died. Ghosts, like memories, defined the past.

Diane sat, as she had done so many times since Moss had come home, and watched sleep overtake him. There were the faint twitchings that no longer alarmed her, part of the healing process, she now realized. She was a part of that process, too, next in line to share his life.

How could she be certain that she and Moss belonged to each other, at least for the time being? The slight pressure of his paw laid claim to her. His ravaged head, heavy in sleep, held her captive on the kitchen floor.

Probably she would never be rid of doubts. But when Moss greeted her anew each morning, she would be as sure as she could be. And Friday afternoons after school started, when she walked up the road, he would be waiting for her.

If Moss knew she would come, if he believed she wouldn't fail him, that would be reward enough for them both.